Creole Folktales

Creole Folktales

by Patrick Chamoiseau

TRANSLATED BY
Linda Coverdale

THE NEW PRESS · NEW YORK

PUBLISHED IN THE UNITED STATES
BY THE NEW PRESS, NEW YORK
DISTRIBUTED BY W. W. NORTON & COMPANY, INC.,
500 FIFTH AVENUE, NEW YORK 10110

ORIGINALLY PUBLISHED IN FRENCH IN 1988
BY EDITIONS HATIER, PARIS.
© 1988 BY PATRICK CHAMOISEAU

LIBRARY OF CONGRESS CATALOGING-IN-PUBLICATION DATA
Chamoiseau, Patrick.
  [Au temps de l'antan. English]
  Creole folktales: au temps de l'antan / Patrick Chamoiseau;
translated by Linda Coverdale.
    p.   cm.
  ISBN 1–56584–185–9
  1. Tales—Martinique.   I. Title.
GR121.M36C5313   1995   94–21475
398.2'097298'2—dc20

PRODUCTION MANAGEMENT BY KIM WAYMER

For Yvan

Damien

Marie-Elodie

Quite properly

and

very simply

The Contents

Introduction: Tales of Survival · *xi*

The Rainmaker · 3

The Most Beautiful One Is Under the Tub · 9

Madame Kéléman · 17

A Pumpkin Seed · 29

Lil' Fellow the Musician · 35

The Person Who Bled Hearts Dry · 49

A Little Matter of Marriage · 55

Glan-Glan, the Spat-Out Bird · 67

Yé, Master of Famine · 75

The Accra of Riches · 85

Ti-Jean Horizon · 91

Nanie-Rosette the Belly-Slave · 101

Beau sang giclé

tête trophée membres lacérés
dard assassin beau sang giclé
ramages perdus rivages ravis

enfance enfance conte trop remué
l'aube sur sa chaîne mord féroce à naître

ô assassin attardé

l'oiseau aux plumes jadis plus belles que le passé
exige le compte de ses plumes dispersées

— AIMÉ CÉSAIRE

Beautiful blood splattered

trophy head slashed limbs
murderous dart beautiful blood splattered
stilled warblings ravished shores

childhood childhood too tumultuous a tale
dawn on its chain snaps ferociously to be born

o foolish assassin

the bird with plumes once more lovely than the past
demands an accounting for its scattered finery

— AIMÉ CÉSAIRE

Introduction: Tales of Survival

O wordsmen of old, masters of the tall story,
tellers of tales around the fire late into the night,
yes, you gatherers of language plucked from the boughs
of despair, I lift up my voice where you left off,
as free and ingenious as you were yourselves.

The seventeenth and eighteenth centuries. In Martinique. First of all, imagine it is nighttime on one of those great sugar cane estates called plantations. The fields are now empty. High on the hill, the lights of a family evening at home in the master's white house have been extinguished by slumber. All are asleep: the manager, the overseers, the European mastiffs, and the little Creole dogs.

At the foot of the hill, in the slave quarters, someone emerges from one of the huts. The slaves are waiting for him, expectantly, beneath an ancient tree. And yet this man seems quite ordinary. He is middle-aged, neither more nor less insignificant than the others. By day, he is merely a field hand who works, suffers, and sweats, living in fear and stifled rebellion.

Perhaps he is even more quietly unobtrusive than most.

At night, however, an obscure and imperative need dispels his lassitude, lifting him up, imbuing him with a nocturnal and almost clandestine force, for he will become the Master of Words.

He is the Storyteller.

Our stories and our Storytellers date from the period of slavery and colonialism. Their deepest meanings can be understood only in relation to this fundamental period in the history of the West Indies. Our Storyteller speaks for a people enchained: starving, terrorized, living in the cramped postures of survival. Their voice is heard in the Creole tale, where the symbolic bestiary of Africa—whale, elephant, tortoise, tiger, brother rabbit—is introduced by the Storyteller to human or supernatural characters of a more distinctly European influence: the Devil, the Goodlord, Cétoute, Ti-Jean Horizon....

While their ludic function is undeniable (for surely laughter is the greatest wellspring of hope for those forced to live in a kind of hell), when taken as a whole, these tales provide a practical education, an apprenticeship in life—a life of survival in a colonized land. The Creole tale says that fear is inevitable, that every blade of grass may conceal a monster, and that one must know how to live with this. The Creole tale reveals that overt force guarantees eventual defeat and punishment, and that through cunning, patience, nerve, and resourcefulness (which is never a sin), the weak may vanquish the strong or seize power by the scruff of the neck. The Creole tale splatters the dominant system of values with all the immoral—or rather, amoral—guile of the poor and downtrodden. Yet these stories contain no "revolutionary" message, and their remedies for misfortune are not collective ones. The hero is alone, and selfishly preoccupied with saving his own skin. And so we might conclude, as Edouard Glissant[1] suggests, that what we have here is an *emblematic detour,* a system of counter-values, or a counterculture, that reveals itself as both powerless to achieve complete freedom and fiercely determined to strive for it nonetheless.

The Creole Storyteller is a fine example of this paradoxical situation: the master knows of his tales and allows him to tell them, and sometimes even listens to them himself, so the Storyteller must take care to use language that is opaque, devious—its significance broken up into a thousand sibylline fragments. His narrative turns around long digressions that are humorous, erotic, often even esoteric. His dialogue with his audience is unceasing, punctuated with onomatopoeias and sound effects intended not only to hold his listeners' attention but also to help camouflage any dangerously subversive content. And here again, Edouard Glissant is right to emphasize that the Storyteller's object is almost *to obscure as he reveals.* To form and inform through the hypnotic power of the voice, the mystery of the spoken word.

When you consider, for example, that it took a law, a statute, a ministerial memorandum, and a gubernatorial decree (1845–46)[2] to persuade the French Béké masters to distribute a few pounds of manioc flour and two or

---

1. Edouard Glissant, *Le Discours antillais,* Editions du Seuil, 1980.
2. Aimé Césaire, "Introduction au folklore martiniquais," *Tropiques* 4, 1941.

three tail ends of codfish to each of their slaves every week, you can readily understand why hunger figures as a constant torment in our Creole tales, which obsessively depict food as the most precious of treasures.

Once the tale is told, our Storyteller is quick to make fun of himself, to show that he is a mere nobody, an outsider even to the people in his story: "They gave me a swift kick in the backside and I trotted on over here to tell you all about it...."

So! In tribute to this stratagem, I did not try to strip the tales you are about to read of all their mystery, nor did I append a glossary. Allow the strange words to work their secret magic, and above all, read these stories only at night. Remember, I wrote them with the moon as my sole companion, for fear of being changed into a basket without handles—a fate described by the old Storytellers, who must have been amused even then to know that I would never, oh never, tempt such a fate as that, just to see....

— PATRICK CHAMOISEAU

Creole Folktales

The Rainmaker

Listen:

In the days of yesteryear, life still blossomed now and again into a kind of dreamworld. Storytellers thus were free to lavish upon their creations liberties that had nothing to do with lies. For instance, they told us of a dismal drought, and of a child who could call down the rain.

Now, the sun had gone way beyond obstinate. The hills had cracked open, releasing the wispy steam of dead roots. The sky had a metallic sheen so bright the slightest cloud committed suicide on the spot. The reddest flowers had burst into flames with sulfurous sighs, while the others—white, yellow, orange—had dried into ocher straw that tickled the nostrils of the oxen, mules, goats, and hens that gathered in exhaustion to mourn the passing of once-gushing springs. There was not a hint of dampness anywhere at all. Complete catastrophe! Folks were going up into the mountains to fetch a sad little dribble of water for their babies' bottles or to moisten the holy oil of the Dominican fathers, which had congealed inside its crystal vials. And, although I'd hate to upset you, I might just add that people had dug up petrified yams, picked stony oranges, plucked guavas that crumbled to dust, and gathered mangoes charred in the secret furnace of dried-up tears.

When the Dominicans discovered that their good wine had turned into a sludge of vinegar, they feared the island had been cursed. They sounded the tocsin throughout the parish, and a pretty sorry lot of wretches answered the call: wild-eyed fishermen, field hands as parched as tree bark, hobbling old-timers whose hides were deeply scored with wrinkles, women with clutches of strangely silent children. The alarm bell also rousted out the Békés, the white colonials with their big parasols. They had changed their ankle boots for rope sandals, unbuttoned their collars, rolled up their sleeves. The women tried to foil the suffocating heat by wearing lace so airy it was hardly there at all. In spite of their verandas and their cisterns, they were oh-so-pale because the heat had spoiled the half-light of their bedrooms, crackled their china, and crazed their looking glasses. High atop their hills, they had gazed through their shutters day after day, hoping for a breeze and watching their wealth shrivel up in the scorching brazier of the cane fields.

When the populace had gathered round, the Dominican fathers told them all to pray for rain. So they prayed to everyone the heavens had to offer in the way of saints, martyrs, gods, the sons of gods and their mothers too, cousins included. They even invoked names unsanctified by any religion, and many a mischievous devil was inadvertently dragged heavenward through their rampant fervor. Not a single raindrop fell. "Ooo," cried the Dominicans, "we are lost!" And they all burst into tears.

Then a child stepped forward, a boy no taller than a hibiscus hedge and wearing rags of sackcloth pieced together with string. "*Kijan lavalas zot lé-a, an brital o an flo?*" he asked the good fathers. "What kind of rain would you like, a frog-choker or just drizzle?" Everyone, black and white, began to sling muddy insults at this cheeky brat: Punish his insolence! Chastise his parents! Call down curses on his descendants! Oh, how could he make sport of their misery that way! But the good fathers said nothing, ladies and gentlemen, for they could clearly see a full-moon innocence in the child's big round eyes, which glimmered like stars in a reflecting pool at the soft approach of a storm. They asked him his name. The child stood mum. The fathers lifted him up onto a barrel and asked him about his parents. An old woman stepped shakily forward to explain that although the boy was not her son, she had been taking care of him in her hut ever since the beginning of Lent, when she had found him loitering around a seven-crossroads. And then she added, "He most strange." In reply to every probing question, the child offered only rain, a lot or a little. So, just for a laugh and without taking him seriously, one of the good fathers said, "We'll take the small size...."

A choice he and the entire community regretted straightaway, down through sixteen generations, for almost one hundred and ninety-nine years, and come every Lent. Because the child brought forth from his rags three

🌱 7 🌱

mysteriously plump oranges. Placing them on the ground where they shone like seashells, he prostrated himself before them, murmuring words in a tongue unknown throughout the Caribbean. The boy stuck a twig into each fruit, accompanying these mysteriously precise gestures with a rambling homily. A froth of spittle edged his lips. When he picked up a single orange and looked toward the sea, a tiny gray cloud sprang into view. Pointing a twig at it, the child patiently drew the cloud closer until it floated overhead. And now a fine, diaphanous, languid rain refreshed the region. The straw huts of the populace and the gutters of the Békés' great houses gleamed wetly; shriveled fruits glistened as if varnished, as did the uplifted faces of the ecstatic crowd. Then the rain trickled away into the droughty earth, sucked up by its great thirst. When the dust-devils returned, and the sun beat down upon them cruelly once again, the people begged the child, "Oh, give us a huge downpour!" But the boy simply gazed at them with the pure candor of a babe in arms.

The Dominicans wrote all this down in a report submitted to their authorities: throughout the entire sun-scorched island, only their parish had enjoyed that brief shower, and even when the rainy season returned, the little town in question never received more than the odd light sprinkle, regardless of the people's desperate need. Even today, this place, called Prêcheur, is as hopelessly dry as an old woman's dugs. The boy lived on there in seclusion and died overcome by threats and entreaties, since he was no longer able to capture even a cloudlet. For it is indeed true that wherever rank bad luck has taken root, a rainmaker may work his miracle only once, and never again.

The Most Beautiful One
Is Under the Tub

Oh,
even
birdbrained words
will
have
their
day,

especially if there is a bird involved. It so happened that off in some corner of the country, when the Devil was just a little boy, there was a parrot that had stopped talking. While all the other wildlife was chattering merrily away, our parrot could only grumble, "*O, lapli bel anba la bay!*," "The most beautiful one is under the tub!" Which didn't make any sense, and everyone said the poor bird had gone dotty with age. So they forgave him his daily commotion of wing-flapping and useless squawking:

> *Lapli bel anba la bay!*
> *Lapli bel anba la bay!*
> *Lapli bel anba la bay!*

This seemed to amuse the bird. A good thing, too, because he was the only one. Well, there came a time when those words took on a meaning, and it was a fine lesson in patience for whenever a mystery seems to be taking too much time. In the bird's neighborhood stood a shack belonging to a mama and her two daughters. The first girl was named Armansia: an ill-mannered little thing with tiny eyes, a teeny mouth, and teensy ears, but the biggest of bad tempers. This, as you know, leads to pimples but not to great beauty. The other daughter, however, was a *real* beauty, by which I mean that she had so much heart and soul that her face simply glowed. Her name was Anastasia. She was as graceful as a swaying coconut palm. She walked the way the wind dances through the sweet-grass. Her mother did not love her at all, however, for she remembered the terrible day of her baptism, when a she-devil appeared among us.

I must admit, that was the only baptism I was never sorry to have missed. Not because they skimped on the food (I'm told they served lashings of fish, a generous spread of potted meats, and the customary roast chickens), and not because the music wasn't lively enough (seventeen drums and a fine array of pipes), but only because a lovely lady turned up at the appointed hour wearing a dress of red madras complicated with antique laces, flounces, and jewels that reflected a light from bygone days. As her garments dragged along the ground, the color of the lush grass changed ever so slightly....

Well, everyone is welcome at a christening party, so despite her strange air, the lovely lady was greeted effusively. She wanted to see the baby. She took Anastasia in her arms, rocked her, kissed her, ran long fingernails through her hair, and put her down again. Then the lady asked to wash her dusty feet. They brought her a basin, which she covered with the hem of her dress. While she was soaking her feet in the water, people could hear the click-click-click of something hard against the edge of the basin, but no one paid any attention, and why spoil the party, anyway? The lovely lady took some refreshments, danced a few *hautes-tailles,* and showed off her pretty teeth in crystalline laughter. At dawn, she repeated her ceremony over Anastasia, but no one noticed, because rum and exhaustion had done them all in. They noticed her leave, though, because from beneath her dress came the sound of a galloping horse. Eyelids bounced open at the sight of her skirts lifting as she showed off (with loud braying) the dun hoofs fetchingly attached to her ankles. A she-devil, if you please! (Oh, that kind of christening party is not for me!) She vanished into a tree—from which burst that silly parrot, squalling his nonsense:

Lapli bel anba la bay!
Lapli bel anba la bay!
Lapli bel anba la bay!

Seeing a she-devil at your daughter's baptism does nothing to foster feelings of motherly love. Thus the mama at first distrusted Anastasia, then feared her, and finally hated her. And she made her life a little slavery: the child lugged charcoal, swallowed clouds of smoke tending the fire, scrubbed the bottoms of pots black since forever, did the family washing at the river, and worked in the fields (weeding, raking, sowing, digging in the yam patch, staying out in the cane fields at cutting time). Not a life to envy—better her than me! Especially since the work seemed to make her beautiful, yes, more beautiful, oh, beauti-beauti-beautiful. The mama, who was not improving with age (and neither was her favorite daughter), only hated that child all the more.

The day of destiny arrived. (I was going to say, here's the beauty part.) Anastasia was out weeding some carrot seedlings, picking her way carefully along the tender green furrows. Even though she was sweaty and tired, she was singing one of those songs that pluck at the heartstrings. Hearing her voice, a young man on horseback turned aside to listen. When he saw her, he thought, "She is the most beautiful girl!" (Oh, the truth is often trite!) He went over to Anastasia, who looked up to see a handsome fellow dressed all in white linen, wearing a hat and boots, with the good manners of a true gentleman. He presented her with a bouquet of hibiscus that blossomed from the hollow of his hand. "*Lapli bel, ki non a'w?*" he asked. "O most beautiful one, what is your name?" Anastasia told him. Then they spent the rest of the day discussing carrots, smiling at each other, and trying out some light caresses. No one knows what he spoke about to her in the way of travels, what dazzling vistas he opened up within her soul, but we do know that he spoke to her and to very good effect. Finally, he found out exactly where she lived and promised to stop by and see her. The gentleman rode off in a cloud of shimmering dust.

Tingling with happiness, Anastasia went home. The twinkle in her clear eye and that little extra something in her beauty put her mama on the alert. She questioned

Anastasia, who told her all about the wonderful stranger and his promised visit. The mama had the feeling there was a wedding coming their way, and decided (better safe than sorry) that it would be wise to marry off Armansia before her pimples and sour disposition transformed her into a lonely cactus (which in her case, sad to say, was not a mere figure of speech).

The next day, the gentleman came riding up to their door. The horse's hoofs were unshod, and the animal was so graceful that it seemed to move in slow motion, as in a dream. The mama had put fresh whitewash on the front of the little house and new straw on the roof, and she had polished the beaten earth all around with a broom, and she had hustled the laying hens (that were always underfoot) and the two pigs (that loved to lie around the yard all day) discreetly out of sight. She waited on her doorstep with Armansia, who stood stiffly in her starched finery, wearing an overpowering perfume and a none-too-flattering hairdo. Oblivious to all this, the gentleman asked after Anastasia.

"She's a bad girl," griped the mother, "a heartless thing, full of bitterness and bad ways...." Wagging a wicked tongue, she claimed that Anastasia had left the house, and the neighborhood, and was probably tramping along the horizon at that very moment. As soon as the mama shut her mouth up, Armansia shot hers off in a rattle of macaquery that the poor thing took for charm. She led the visitor by the hand to a seat in the shade, offered him coconut milk, and showed him the garden, the pigs, the sheep, and the hens. She even pointed out, I'm told, high on a wall, the star-shaped web of a seven-hundred-year-old spider. The handsome youth considered these marvels with a vacant stare. It was Anastasia's voice he heard in memory, and his mind's eye saw only the landscapes of her laughter, her sparkling gaze, and the natural elegance of the most beautiful girl of all. He soon remounted his horse, which neighed in prolonged sadness. He was already trotting away forever when he heard:

> *Lapli bel anba la bay!*
> *Lapli bel anba la bay!*
> *Lapli bel anba la bay!*

The parrot, as loony as ever, had gone into one of its fits of nonsense. Fluttering awkwardly on tired wings, it hovered with unusual persistence around an overturned tub that ordinarily served as a water trough for the pigs and chickens. Other birds even stopped in midflight to watch the parrot's antics, which so amused them that they joined right in, and now a whirlwind of sarcelles, of timid thrushes, blackbirds, colibris, and eskimo curlews swirled like sparks in a bonfire above the tub. Intrigued (naturally), the gentleman dismounted and, despite the protests of mother and daughter, went over to peek under the tub, where (of course) he found the most beautiful one—bound and gagged by her mama! After a kiss, they never looked back as they galloped off to the fancied delights of unknown destinies. Then the parrot dropped like a falling tear upon the wooden tub, as if free at last from the words this protracted mystery had compelled him to repeat (without understanding a single one of them) for almost twenty years.

Madame Kéléman

Once,
twice,
thrice—
another good story!

I'm going to pick the one about Madame Kéléman. Listen if you want to understand, and you'll hear how a mother who had already run out of luck gave birth to her fourteenth daughter, thus complicating the daily and impossible task of sharing the contents of their empty larder. In an effort to get rid of her youngest without God noticing it, this mama sent her off each morning deep into the dangerous forest in search of items that were useless and, above all, simply not to be found. And so one day she said, "Ho, my girl, go get your mama four sous' worth of butter." She pretended to place four sous into a mango pit (the only change purse the poor can afford in these parts). Without any backtalk, the child took the pit and set off for wherever one would go in the woods to buy a bit of butter. Walking and daydreaming along, she found that she had lost her way and could not find it anywhere ahead, behind, or even in the clear-as-clear-could-be geography of childish reverie. Come nightfall, she came across an old lady, sitting—in that way that only old folks have—beneath a tall fern.

"*Manman ho, an pèd latras,*" said the child. "Mama, I'm lost!" Then the old lady, all honey, led the girl into her woodland hut, a hut made of bone-straw and the feathers of white birds, with a roof of dry coconuts held together by the spittle of webless spiders. Well, this was most definitely the hut of one of those obeah-women who are known elsewhere as witches. But the little girl didn't know anything about this because what she didn't know was way more than what she did. Inside the gloomy hut, the unwavering flame of a candle stub illuminated only a rocking chair, onto which the old lady sat herself down with a creak.

"*Man, fal mwen flo,*" whimpered the child. "Mama, I'm hungry." The crone replied in a voice thickened by flaccid gums, "And me, it's thirsty I am—always thirsty! Why don't you just fetch me a drop of water from the spring, and then I'll give you all the food you want." The girl went off to take the waters (literally) and she took them to the old lady, who poured them down her gullet, gloof! One trip led to another, and another, and the more calabashes the child dragged back, the more water the old lady sucked down, down, down, as though her throat were south of a burning desert. Simply exhausted, the little girl moaned, "I'm hungry, oh, I'm hungry!" The old lady told her, "Oho, my girl, when you've found out mama's name, mama'll give you all you can eat, and some butter, and even show you the right way home! But first things first: find out my name...." And by disappearing she made herself invisible.

The little girl stayed within the dirty glow of the candle as the living shadows in the hut moved all around her, forming and unforming shapes like net curtains twisting in the wind, the shadows of eyeless stares drawn to the shivers on her skin. When the guttering candle sputtered out its last gleams, the child burst into tears, which fell with such distress that a big-Big-BIG serpent emerged from the darkness. Not a snakeling, but a nice, fat, thick snake that came over to her as though it were a pet dog and even rubbed its head against her legs to reassure her (which, I'm telling you, would not have reassured me in the least, but alas, I'm no longer a child!). Then the serpent whispered, "*Ni yonn dé bèt anba bwa-a ki konnèt non'y—fouyé pala.*" "Some forest creatures know her name—go ask them."

Though the hour was late, the little girl went out to comb the woods. Inside cathedrals of bamboo, she questioned twenty-two thousand rats, not one of whom knew the old lady's name. She poked beneath the velvety undersides of leaves, but the dainty anoli lizards had to confess that they didn't know the old lady's name. She climbed custard-apple trees, but the manicou possums only looked up from their nocturnal feasting to apologize for not knowing the old lady's name. And when she waded ankle-deep through the backwater marshes, he-toads and she-toads did not even pause in their acrobatic amours to croak out their ignorance of the old lady's name. And what's more, since we're going into detail here, neither the woodhorses, nor the sizzling fireflies, nor the web-spinners, nor the raucous hummingbirds, nor the blinking stinkbugs, nor the nyah-nyah flies and skeeters, nor even that pesky caterpillar that loves to nurse at women's breasts could tell her the old lady's name.

Quite disheartened, the little girl plopped down by a spring. Now, in those days, crabs lived in these refreshing spots, with their seven crab-wives, their crablet progeny, and inexhaustible swarmings of crabby cousins, godchildren, and godparents. And they were a pretty sight to see, because at the end of their long necks they had pert heads topped with cunning little flat-brimmed boaters with egg-shaped crowns. Oh, they were darling in those days, the crabs, and since their straw hats didn't cover up their ears, they heard all the grapevine gossip, the malicious hearsay, rampant rumors, idle prattle, yackety-yak, all the dirt dished out at funerals, and even what the Frenchy white folks call tittle-tattle and just plain rubbish. Since the truth might easily have gotten lost in all that jabber, the crabs answered the little girl's question with a hearty all-together-now:

> *La Madame Kéléman bradiman Kéléman*
> *La Madame Kéléman bradiman Kéléman*
> *La Madame Kéléman bradiman Kéléman*
> *La Madame Kéléman bradiman Kéléman*

And they sang out this chorus while cutting capers around the spring. The trouble with the crabs was that in spite of their dashing flat-brimmed boaters with the egg-shaped crowns, in spite of their lovely long necks and their regal heads, they had more legs than smarts and more claws than brains. So when the girl asked them as well for a bite to eat, directions for finding her way home, or just a simple word of encouragement, all they replied was:

> *La Madame Kéléman bradiman Kéléman*
> *La Madame Kéléman bradiman Kéléman*
> *La Madame Kéléman bradiman Kéléman*
> *La Madame Kéléman bradiman Kéléman*

The child soon tired of this and returned slowly to the hut. The old lady made her reappearance at dawn, adding the creaking of her bones to the creaking of her rocking chair. "Well, my girl, do you know mama's name?" she quavered. "*An sav*—I know it," murmured the child. The old lady settled herself in that rocker, filled a pipe with tobacco, lit it, pulled from the folds of her dress the thirty chilly mabouya lizards that bring relief from the heat, squeezed her eyes down to slits, and prepared to enjoy the time-honored test that had proved the last undoing of all her other victims. In a soft but vicious voice (the same one she had used seven hundred times seven hundred and seven times six thousand times before) she said, "If you don't say my name, I'm going to eat you on the spot!"

What a fright! The little girl lost her memory and stammered out Charlotte, Jeanne, Geneviève, Thérèse, Armansia, Vovonne, Manotte, Fidéline, Aristophane, Sidonie, and suchlike, to the sinister amusement of the old lady, who no longer bothered to conceal her true nature: a parasitic vine writhed through her hair, her teeth had grown as big and yellow as a cow's, her nails had turned into claws, and her feet—how do you like this?— now displayed a cloven sheath of shining gray horn, which storytellers given to exaggeration would call hoofs. The gluttonous hag was already heaving herself out of the chair when the little girl shouted at dizzying speed:

La Madame Kéléman bradiman Kéléman
La Madame Kéléman bradiman Kéléman
La Madame Kéléman bradiman Kéléman
La Madame Kéléman bradiman Kéléman

Oops! The old lady spun around like a top, jiggling as though tiny flames were blazing all over her body. "You've beaten me, you've beaten me!" In her rage she trampled snakes and mabouyas, tore out fistfuls of her hair, beat her right breast over her heart (she had one, but on the wrong side) and sniveled out some hard little crystals that stung her eyes. She offered the girl everything we like to eat around here: scads of things au gratin, piles of fricassees, rafts of fishes cooked in court-bouillon, and various meaty soups, stews, and roasts. And then she told her, "The house is yours, and all its insides too...."

While the child ate—oh, eating's not the word for it!—Madame Kéléman (yes indeed, it was she, that obeah-woman of vices and saucy sorcery, the chamber-pot crony of more than one old zombi, the Bat King's bedfellow in the buff, practically chief undercook in hell's kitchen, yes, her!) snatched up her ancient cutlass and set out for revenge in the early light of dawn. At her outraged approach, the forest creatures scampered off so briskly—just to avoid cramping her style—that she did not meet so much as an ant along the way, or even the shadow of one. It wasn't until she reached the savanna that she came across a three-horned bull, named Bêf. And without waiting for a court of justice or an attorney at law, she lit right into him. "Hey, Bêf! You're the one! You hear me? You're the one who found out, you're the one who knows, and you're the one who told everybody what I'm called!"

La Madame Kéléman bradiman Kéléman
La Madame Kéléman bradiman Kéléman
La Madame Kéléman bradiman Kéléman
La Madame Kéléman bradiman Kéléman

But Bêf replied, "Not me, I swear! I'm not the one who knows that, really...." Madame Kéléman looked him up and down while he shook his shivers. Just to be mean, she yanked out one of his horns before rushing off again, which is why nowadays bulls have only two. On the other side of the savanna, Madame Kéléman surprised a five-legged mule, called Milé, who'd been so thrilled to be cropping the tender grass of the open plain that he simply hadn't seen her coming. And without benefit of court or attorney, she accused the mule as well. "No no no!" protested Milé, ratta-tat-tat. Repaying his innocence with malice, this Madame Kéléman ripped off one of his legs before going on, which is why, even as we speak, mules are the way they are.

After another sweep through the woods, Madame Kéléman came to the spring where the crabs lived, with their extravagant necks, their pompous heads, and their festive flat-brimmed boaters with the egg-shaped crowns. The crabs were in a tizzy because one of their she-crabs was about to become the mother of a whopping clutch of crablets. All of them were preparing for this happy event, and some were getting ready to go fetch the midwife. Well, as was her wont, without further ado Madame Kéléman started shouting accusations. "Hey, crabs! You're the ones! You hear me? You're the ones who know what I'm called and who told everyone—" But before she could finish, the crabs—enraged at this show of disrespect—shouted back at her, and let the spittle fly. "We're the ones, you hag! We're the ones, you witchy bitch! Yes, we did it, you silly set of toothless gums! We're the ones who blabbed around the song about your name!"

La Madame Kéléman bradiman Kéléman
La Madame Kéléman bradiman Kéléman
La Madame Kéléman bradiman Kéléman
La Madame Kéléman bradiman Kéléman

And they danced a frenetic calenda that gave Madame Kéléman fits of weepy fury, the kind that smoothes out wrinkles (by making your face all puffy) but gives you white hairs. Madame Kéléman raised her cutlass with its blade of misfortune, honed sharp upon the grindstone of disaster, and slammed the flat side down—thwack!—on the jolly crabs. Oh, shed a tear! That cut their song short. Their flat-brimmed egg-crowned boaters were jammed all the way down their long necks, and their noble heads, so proudly held on high, were sadly squashed into whatever was left. Which is why crabs, to this day, are headless.

Despite this devastation, the crabs continued to proclaim in broad daylight the name of Madame Kéléman. The echo of their voices skimmed through the undergrowth, clambered up the evergreen filao trees, and from there launched itself toward an endless firmament of ears: gossips, rumormongers, tattletales, and those detestable souls who write (and rewrite) stories that tap out a tempting tattoo on their eardrums. Madame's name became so well known that she felt she would never again be able to force lost travelers to bring her water by subjecting them to that hoary riddle. It seems that somewhere inside her, too much chagrin got mixed up with too much self-pity and too much gassy wrath, which made her tripple—a Creole way of saying that she tripped in a heartwarmingly spectacular fashion. She hit the ground so hard it opened up like a well-thumbed book of suffering, and snapped shut on her like a bible of fate. This place on earth became most unwholesome, and there sprouted forth a spiny horror, a plant the Békés called "no escape," which they cultivated in the days of slavery.

Now, Madame Kéléman disappeared just as the little girl was finishing her meal. When the charms surrounding her exploded into fiery plumes of sparks, the light they gave off was something marvelous to see. The straw, bones, and feathers of that hut turned into sweet-smelling wood of a kind that grows only in Guiana, and now the hut was beautiful. The toads changed into more little girls, all warbling joyously, while the mabouyas and small-fry snakes swelled up into startled boys, who stood blinking at the onrush of their belated dreams. As for everything else, great riches took its place: patches of everlasting yams and groves of blue breadfruit trees, crystallized tears with the promise of diamonds, seeds of fertility, a pile of money swindled from Madame Kéléman's victims, ka-drums all resonant with ancestral memory, and forgotten Creole words that Madame Kéléman had clapped into calabashes so that she might listen to them with intoxicated delight. The little girl, they say, lived a happily-ever-after life with the big serpent, who turned into quite a fine fellow. Everyone is so welcome in their home that even vagabonds like me stop by there after story-time to raise a glass in honor of the lovely lady of the house.

A Pumpkin Seed

They tell the
story of an old woman
who—despite wrinkles,
the sufferings of
age, the stings
of ingrati-
tude,
and
even loneliness—was still all heart.

Some people are like that: they are made of goodness, their every look spreads tenderness, and from their hands caresses fall all the year round. This elderly lady lived in chinpontong, a Creole way of saying she was up the crick and stony-broke. Her hut was of straw. Her pallet was stuffed with dried grass. Her only valuable was a little bottle of camphorated rum for soothing her aches and pains. She ate watercress, and more water-cress, and didn't even have enough strength left to run her fingers beneath the rocks of the riverbed to look for those crawfish we call zabitan. So she was famine's best friend, which proves without a doubt that a friendship is not necessarily one of life's true pleasures.

One fine morning the old lady went toddling off into the undergrowth to collect twigs of logwood, which make such crackling fires. She was going along when all of a sudden, she spied a thrashing of wings in a tuft of rank grass. It wasn't a colibri, or a little blackbird, or a robin redbreast, or a sunbird, or a yellow cici warbler.... It was a small bird that had never been named by the

Creole tongue, and as for this language, it has no idea such a thing even exists. The bird was wounded. Cradling it at her breast, the old lady hurried back to her hut. And though she had not tasted meat, or chewed a morsel of chicken, or sucked on a marrow bone in many a day, she now thought only of nursing the creature: pouring a drop of camphorated rum on the tiny wound and a sip of sugarwater into the parched beak, stroking the feathers, singing lullabies, snuggling up the quilted cotton bedjacket to ward off the chill of fear. When it was time to eat, she ate her watercress. She ate it the next day as well, and the day after, and all the other days that followed. Caring and attentive, she fed the bird as best she could, bestowing such tenderness upon the patient that each night it fell asleep against her cheek or tucked into one of the deep hollows behind her collarbones. When she had restored the bird to health, she returned it to the forest, to the very same spot where she had found it. There she waited—with a heavy heart—until it flew jauntily away. Then she went back to the sorrows of her hut, and to the fresh sorrow of the bird's departure.

She did not see it again until some time later, when she was grazed by a wingtip as she stooped crookedly to pluck her midday watercress. It was the bird. It soared over the hut and swooped to lay a pumpkin seed at her feet. Then off it flew, caroling happiness. The old lady planted the seed in her own tender way, sprinkling it daily with water warmed by a loving heart. Me, with all that attention, I would have sprung up in no time. The pumpkin didn't wait to be asked: sprout, stalk, leaves, flowers, and first fruit. A pretty pumpkin, hefty, with a nice oval shape. Oh, a pleasure beyond words: the old lady harvesting her first pumpkin, all aquiver to think of escaping that watercress for once. She had neither salt nor spices, but so what—a dish of pumpkin would be tasty, yes sirree! She picked it the way one would pick babies if they grew on trees. On the table, she opened it up.... Oh! Inside the pumpkin was a fully cooked meal: a ragout of good meat and rice, garnished with a sprig of parsley. Her feast lasted only as long as three mouthfuls, for those nibblings of watercress had shrunk her stomach down to the merest memory of itself. But what a banquet! The first mouthful infused her body with all the aromas of her youth. The second was bursting with every forgotten flavor. The third seemed to fill the aching of her bones, the murmurs of her heart. She was satisfied.

To avoid wasting the leftovers, she carried them to her closest neighbor, a very ordinary person whose only property was a pepper plant, which she guarded fiercely. This neighbor tucked in heartily, giving thanks with loud cries. Then she wanted to see this wonder-working pumpkin up close. Every day, at noontime, the vine produced a big fruit stuffed with different things to eat (sometimes there was even chocolate sherbet). The sweet old lady, without one word of complaint, saw her friendship with famine come to an end. She went on with her life in a kind of bliss, with the occasional bite of watercress just for old times' sake. But the neighbor, even though she benefited from this godsend, schemed and schemed and schemed, bug-eyed with envy.

Since the old lady had told her the story many a time,

the neighbor set out on purpose to do her own good deed. She looked beneath leaves and between roots for the sick bird with the broken wing and the beak stilled by suffering. Nothing! Only lovely birds in the pink of health perched plumb upon their branches. Enraged, she snatched up a stone and brought down a victim. It wasn't a colibri, or a little blackbird, or a robin redbreast, or a sunbird, or a cici…. It was you've-already-guessed-what. She carried it home, poured a bit of gutter water on the wound, plopped the poor thing down on a dirty rag, and went off for a nap. The next morning, in a great hurry, she tossed the birdy into a passing breeze, which it caught as best it could, dragging one wing behind.

Our neighbor now began to scan the skies, watching for that seed. Sure enough, it arrived. The bird flung it at her without even slowing down. The neighbor planted it, watered it, screeched out some songs for it, and so the pumpkin vine, after stalk leaves and flowers, produced its first fruit. The neighbor split it right open, licking her lips. Oh! Out sprang a hellish mob of snakes, spiders, skinks, and fat brown mabouyas, all under the unfortunate impression that she was their mother. Their cold maws gaping, they lunged for her breasts. Ladies and gentlemen, the neighbor clapped a hand on her head, took to her heels, and sped off as fast as her legs could carry her. No one knows how she got on board, but in the end she sailed away on a wind that never came back.

Lil' Fellow the Musician

Are you all asleep?

No?

Then so far, so good!

Well, it's a fine thing to have self-confidence, but you mustn't overdo it, because with too much confidence you can outsmart yourself. An old story reminds frogs who puff themselves up with importance of the misfortune that befell the marvelous little musician fellow we knew from hereabouts. This child was born at the very moment when a hurricane was sighing its last. The baleful blast prowled around above the village, turning the sky gray, pollarding the trees, seething like a smashed-open anthill. Sometimes it brushed against a cliff, echoing to the tune of a melancholy waltz. At other times, it streamed through groves of straw-colored bamboo, sun-baked with great age, and set them rustling with fibrous melodies. Sucking on their pipes in the doorways of their huts, the old men watched all this with eyes like glittering pebbles. They lowered their gaze only to admit among themselves, with an uneasy pleasure, that this wind was one fine musician: "*Van tala sé mizik....*"

One day, they got out the drums, unwrapped a few fiddles, and brought back from oblivion the mandolins of yesteryear. Clambering to the top of a bluff, they played cadences in honor of the wind. This made a kind of music that no musician (even when inspired by tafia) had ever imagined. O music of the earth, the sea, and the sky! Flights of birds provided vibrant solos. Celebrant insects trilled the refrain. Everywhere, folks from the towns or countryside, wearing perfume or simply sweaty, set themselves to dancing, oh, to dancing, yes, to dancing, in bold despite of the vicissitudes of life. But, in the time it has taken me to tell you all that, the boy grew up, and they called him Lil' Fellow. No sooner was his ear opened then he heard the music. "*Mantyé yo pipo-a,*" he said to his parents. "They need a flute." In no time Lil' Fellow picked the proper bamboo, made the proper holes in it, did all the proper things you need to do anywhere to make a proper flute. He joined the old musicians up on the bluffs. The sounds he made were soon written on the concert of the wind. O beauty! The hurricane's last sigh lost all its sadness. It whirled with new life, bumped aside a score of clouds, and went on its way the way hurricanes do—in a hurry.

The music and dance from this business stayed on, however. People heaped honors upon Lil' Fellow, giving him the title of musician. Then, the greatest of musicians. Then, Maestro. Then, some other such silliness. So Lil' Fellow forgot that he was only as old as one rainstorm and two mango seasons. He also forgot that his ignorance was bigger than he was. What I mean is, things came to such a pass that he even disobeyed his parents. When they said starboard, he veered to port. When they played a beguine, he danced a mazurka. To snuff out any punishment, he had only to flourish his flute and pipe a tune. All anger died away, scowls vanished, and clenched fists opened to beat a peaceful tempo—instead of him.

Lil' Fellow the musician was untouchable. He thought himself invincible. Well, here's the thing: It so happened that he and his parents had gone far into the forest to dig for wild yams, and they were late in starting back home. The shadows were lengthening already. Now, the woods around here are a gateway to hell, so his parents told him to run for his very life. Which they themselves proceeded to do. As they disappeared into the distance, his parents begged him not to disobey them this one time. "*Saki pé lévé lan min douvan mizik mwen an?*" he replied. "Who could ever resist my music?" And not one step did he run. And he even dawdled, turning a haughty eye upon the gathering dusk.

Soon darkness was everywhere. The darkness of deep in the forest where nothing is ever still, so eagerly do the spirits of the next life strive to return to this one. Lil' Fellow was strolling along without even realizing that the glowworms watching him go by could also see what lay ahead. He almost died when he ambled around a clump of tall grass to find a horse with huge horns barring his path. The touch of the flute in the hollow of his hand reassured him. He waited. Motionless. He knew it was no use running from any creature with more than two feet. Even the glowworms had gone out. The faint breeze that tickles leaves had stolen away. The only things left were silence and silence, darkness and darkness, and vice versa. "*La ou sôti, ti mal?*" asked the horse casually. "Where have you come from, little boy?" The animal also remarked that it was time for all good children to be home in their mothers' huts. Lil' Fellow lifted the bamboo flute to his lips and blew:

> *Péla man lou, Péla man li*
> *Péla man li, Péla man lou*
> *Corali belli, corali belli*
> *Péli péla péli péla*
> *Plam!*

Oh, the horse wept to hear such music! Behind those tears glittered twinkles of joy, or perhaps it was contentment. Which proves that the creature wasn't really evil in spite of its coat of feathers, its webbed hoofs, its corkscrewy fishtail, and its countless horns, for truly, when a horse gets it into its head to have horns, there's no stopping it. Finally it spoke again, sounding much refreshed. "*Pasé monfi, mé lapli bel anba la bay.*" "Pass, my son, but the best is yet to come."

I'd be lying if I said that after this encounter, Lil' Fellow walked on. It was more like a gallop. Flat out. Barely a hundred yards farther along, he ran into some kind of hot and fetid wind, a stale stink of rancid frypans and withered flowers. Coming straight at him were eyes of fire like torches on a citadel. He saw a calamity of flesh, scales, and horny hide, in a yellowish cloud of sulfur and flickering flames. Sometimes this sort of thing is called a dragon, but whatsoever it's called, the effect remains the same. "*O ou sôti, ti mal?*" screamed the calamity. "Where have you come from, little boy?" It also shouted that it was time for all good children to be home in their mothers' huts. Without replying, Lil' Fellow showed he was a champion of sang-froid by managing to bring the bamboo flute to his lips and blow:

Péla man lou, Péla man li
Péla man li, Péla man lou
Corali belli, corali belli
Péli péla péli péla
Plam!

Oh, the calamity showed some very lovely teeth. It lit up in delight. Its little flames smoked with pleasure. With its abysmal nostrils, it sniffed in Lil' Fellow's milky smell. The desire to gulp him down was greasing its tongue. All the same, charmed by the music, it said, "Pass, my son, but the best is yet to come...."

How shall I put it? Lil' Fellow took off, yes! His heels flying about his ears, his eyes popping from their sockets, his arms flapping like wings, yes, he ran! But run as he might (and as fast as running can be written), he could not outrun his fate. Everything crackled on all sides: trees, branches, dappled shadows, hulking darknesses, and scraps of gray. It sounded like a few dozen volcanoes, a racket in which one could sometimes hear the snapping of twigs that were probably of no great importance. What did he see before him as clearly as I would have seen you had you been there? What did he see, ho? What did he see, this presumptuous pup, this pighead who seemed like a mule even though his ears were nothing special? Hmm?

The Seven-Headed Beast.

Fourteen eyes of lightning and thunder. Teeth of needles, thicker than tree trunks, longer than bamboo stalks, yellower than jaundice. A tail that wrapped seven times around the belly before snaking off for another seven leagues. Ooo, no mistake about that one! Instead of a heart, a dab of grease. Just the shadow of an impossibility for a soul. And no more feeling than one of those waves out on the ocean. The Beast took a turn around Lil' Fellow. Looked him up. Looked him down. Looked at him askance, then right in the face. In a chorus of seven voices it grunted, "Where have you come from, little boy? This is the hour when serpents frolic in the woods, when zombies are abroad, when all good children are home in their mothers' huts...." But Lil' Fellow was already piping away as he had never piped before, even summoning up in his flute that cyclonic sigh he had set free once upon a time. O divine music! O nectar to the ears! The Seven-Headed Beast drank in this harmony with tears in all its eyes, and even sweated with pleasure, allowing this flush to pass before opening its seven jaws, sticking out its seven tongues, and swallowing our Lil' Fellow down its single throat—guwulp! That old Beast had a taste more for meat than for music. I'm told it still roams the forest and that people remember it from time to time, but as for Lil' Fellow, he is more forgotten today than the palmettos that once grew in the caldera of Mount Pelée.

The Person Who Bled
Hearts Dry

THEY SAY THAT IN THE DAYS OF
THE SLAVE TRADE, MORE THAN ONE SEA CAPTAIN HAD HIS TROUBLES. THERE'S NO CALL TO SHED TEARS OVER THEM, BUT ALLOW ME TO TELL YOU ABOUT THE TRADER WHO TRANSPORTED, IN HIS HOLD, A PERSON OF A MOST TERRIBLE SORT. (THIS CAPTAIN'S NAME IS NOT WORTH WRITING DOWN—STILL LESS THAT OF HIS SHIP.)

As he was homeward bound from the shores of Africa, where the sinister harvests of ebony were gathered in, his crew informed him that three sailors had wasted away in a peculiar fashion, without fever or pain; their blood simply seemed to fall stagnant, thickening into dark honey. That very day, one of the captives in the cargo died in the same manner. The worried captain had the bodies lined up hard by the mainmast, then looked them over and said, "Let's see what shape their hearts are in…." Rooting around in their chests, the ship's surgeon—a man of the Church who had undoubtedly drowned his soul in the sacramental wine—found only four wrinkled guavas, stunted and sere like some tropical scrub, and no one would ever have taken them for hearts if they hadn't been sitting in the right spot. Feeling faint, our captain had all this lot pitched over the side, heave-ho: four little splishes and four big splashes! The ship went on its dreadful way.

As the meantime went by, there were more clusters of

these mysterious deaths, among both sailors and slaves, that no prayer seemed able to stem. Four to port, seven to starboard, not to mention those abeam and abaft— off the bodies went to the tag-along dogfish. Sensing that his harvest was in danger, or that his men were slipping into mutiny, the captain had the most trembly of the trembling slaves brought to his cabin. "What is causing this disaster?" he demanded. "Answer, or our sharks will snap you up alive!" Just before his blood turned to syrup, the wretch blurted out, "The old woman with rings on her fingers—she feeding herself that way...." Then he died. They tossed him to the voracious fish he had so hoped to avoid (and I think we can say that this must have annoyed him, all the same).

Our captain sent for this beringed crone, and from the hold they fetched a woman of uncertain age, quite old, quite young, all dusty with ancient years and all in a childish flutter. "Where does she come from?" asked the captain, "and who brought her to us?" This was a puzzle. The mate, leader of the ruffians who raided peaceful villages to capture young slaves, had never seen her among his ropes and nets. As for the bosun's mate who haggled over the black gold of the coastal barracoons, he could not recall trading her for I-don't-know-what glass trinket or pouch of tobacco. And none of the armorer's mates remembered putting any chains on her. And no one in the galley had noticed her uplifted face waiting for the foul soup they dished out every day. It was such an odd business that the captain chewed it over with a very bad grace for three hours, until the creature spat in his eye, shrieking words from an Africa beyond the reach of time. Although he felt some vague misgivings, the captain ordered her taken out on deck.

There, before the captives assembled amid vinegar fumes intended to mask the stench, he had her whipped, lashed to a gun, flogged for longer than it would take me to write it out ten thousand times. It was a mere shred the surgeon treated with bayberry and salt, in the shade of a longboat. And yet, the shred summoned the strength to hoist herself up on one elbow and point a quivering finger at the captain, a black finger, but white with infinite malediction. The strange person did not, of course, survive the remedies dispensed by the man of the Church. They say that after her corpse was flung overboard, the sharks veered and sheered all around without ever touching her, and so she floated for one hundred and twenty-five years, until her sea-change into a tragedy of coral that terrifies medusas.

As for the captain, they claim that all sleep deserted him the first night, that on the second one he wept to feel his memories fading away, and that on the third, his blood thickened into a sugar as dense as carbon, clotting around his suddenly dried-up heart. At the sight of his lifeless body, the crew gave themselves up for damned, and began to dance upon the deck, upon the helm, upon the astrolabe and portolanos, upon the shrouds and the tangling sails. They danced so much that this shitty ship met with some misfortune (or maybe a coral reef) and plummeted to the scrapey bottom of the ocean deeps, surfacing only in the company of other phantom vessels, the only ships that warned the sleepless slave traders that their human ferocity secreted in its own heart atrocities more savage still.

A Little Matter of Marriage

I saw this tale
go past my hut
in the small hours
of a sunny night;
a big dream had left me
with little insomnias,
and my hut finally up and quit
this time for another
where time was lost
and tempest-tossed.
I left my hut in time,
for I had a mind
to take the time
to tell you this story
about a marriage
that came to an untimely end,
but which tonight
will help us
pass the time
in style.

Ladies and gentlemen, there was once a girl of marriageable age. Her mother was a strong woman; life had furrowed her brow without managing to bow her shoulders. So, she lived in her shanty with a daughter named Tétiyette, and a big boy who had no name, and a second boy whose name has been lost, and a third little boy so crippled and ugly that no one had thought to name him at all (which wasn't so terrible, because around these parts, ladies and gentlemen, the names can be rather nasty). This last child drooled so much, by the way, that his mother had built him a tiny *ajoupa* out in the front yard. There he lived both day and night, because his brothers (and his sister in particular) would not allow him in their home. The ugly boy spent his time cultivating some idiotic bushes with no leaves, no fruit, and just a few gray flowers at the tips of their scrawny branches. He tended them as carefully as the crabs dig their holes at the approach of Easter. He sprinkled his charges with tepid water, rubbed their bark with oily rags, meticulously trimmed any infected twig-ends, and did so with such love that his infirmities took on a kind of grace. Sometimes his family even caught him talking to the bushes and, stranger yet, listening attentively as though they were talking back to him. So, everyone finally decided the ugly boy was *toktok*, which is Creole for crazy.

Well, as I was saying, Tétiyette was pronounced ready for marriage when her mother noticed how she seemed to glow with a quivering radiance. Her budding prettiness had blossomed into beauty, a beauty as fascinating to the eye as the dew is to dragonflies in the cool of the morning. And to her suitors she was lovely, more lovely than the rumor of rain conjured up by thirsty foliage during a drought, and more lovely than the pearly intimacy within the convolutions of a shell, and (to be precise) as lovely as the salty glitter of the sea when the sun beats down with impossible heat, hammering it smooth. More than one suitor moaned, and myself loudest among them, "O light of her beauty, O!" Unfortunately, the beauty herself finally realized this and began putting on airs, sashaying her backbone around like a wriggling snake, so stuck-up her long eyelashes dripped with disdain: no one was good enough for her! This person was too fat. That person was too bony. So-and-so thought way too highly of himself, while all and sundry looked to her like hairy beasts, namely those banana-eaters that swing about on vines. People say she actually turned down an imposing man of solid gold astride a black horse, and refused to cast even the slightest flicker of a glance at a lively fellow made of silver sitting on the cushions of a glass wheelbarrow, and (which is why I never dared show her my face) she gave short shrift to a gentleman all of diamond perched on a red horse and sparkling like a sapphire from Brazil.

The suitors came thick and fast. As guardian of the door, the ugly boy announced each one, but in vain. Rejected, they slunk shamefully away. Then—a most unusual thing—the ugly boy drew near a window of the shanty, and called to his sister. "*Tétiyette, sésé, pwan gad,*" he said. "Sister Tétiyette, watch out." His family was struck not so much by the warning as by his fleecy, wispy voice, which seemed almost to evaporate from his lips in a way they had never heard before. The mama shed a tear of troubled joy. "*Piti tala enmen nou,*" she thought. "This child loves us...."

One day, when a dainty sun-shower was falling, some-one appeared at their front gate, which the ugly boy opened in silence, his eyes downcast, and without his usual street-vendor's cry to announce the newcomer. This visitor was long-limbed, clothed in white drill, wearing a hat, and carrying a slender cane, as elegant as a night beneath an April moon. Silence enveloped him like a mosquito net. From her window, Tétiyette saw a handsome white man who was powerfully and seductively unsettling. He asked for a bowl of water, which he drank without moving his throat. Then he said, "I've heard, dear lady, that you have a daughter of marriageable age." Ill at ease, the mama pointed to the window where Tétiyette, leaning on her elbows, was watching fondly. "Show him in, Mama," said the girl with a smile.

This done, they sat at the table and spoke of this and that—the sea, the wind, birds' eyelids when the rain falls slantwise, the curving fingernails of a centenarian woman, the flesh of a boxfish rubbed with spices and baked in hot ashes, the slightly lemony taste of the succulent julie-mango, and how a blind man sees a rainbow in his mind's eye. Then, from who knows where, he produced for her an immortelle, a porcelain rose, a flowering liana of turquoise jade, and four of those ephemeral flowers called hibiscus. He made her see the month of May in a branch of the coral tree, the rainy season in the frangipani, Lent in the cassia, and the sweet joys of Noel in the poinsettia. Finally, just before proposing marriage, he offered her a bird-of-paradise, an orchid that is the insolence of our gardens.

Well, naturally, Tétiyette said yes, as happy as an ortolan on toast. The man immediately set the date of the wedding. Before leaving, he gave the mama a bag of silver, enough to pay for festivities that would haunt everyone's dreams. Despite her misgivings, the mama was pleased at this, so she kissed Tétiyette and her two brothers, and they cavorted around the chairs and up on the table. Then the ugly boy's face loomed in the window, and in the indecipherable tragedy of the cripple's eyes, Tétiyette could vaguely perceive love, sorrow, pity. Seized with compassion, she embraced him as well, allowing his drool to smear her cheek. "*Tétiyette sésé, ban mwen an favè*," said her little brother. "Sister Tétiyette, do me a favor." Tétiyette agreed. The ugly boy handed her a thorn from one of his bushes, begging her to prick her future husband with it on the first possible occasion. "*Si sé san ki bay, ibon, mé si sé nannan, bay kouri*," he whispered to her. "If blood spurts out, that's fine, but if it's something else, run away quickly!" Without understanding too clearly, his big sister gave him her promise.

At her fiancé's next visit, while they were figuring out how much food they would need for the wedding feast, Tétiyette pricked her future husband without him noticing it. (No need to be astonished: any woman can steal your heart without opening your chest!) So anyway, during one of those tender moments alone that lovers know how to arrange, she pricked him, releasing a flow of something that smelled of stagnant water. However (I'm not exaggerating: love and reason are two different things, and they had a falling out over some cheating at dice in a game of serbi) she said nothing of this to anyone, especially not to the ugly boy, who looked at her questioningly with disaster in his gaze.

The marriage was celebrated by an unknown priest: he had no church, he had no cross, he had no gown, nor even any Latin, but his azure eyes were enough to dazzle us, I think, so that we saw him as a bishop, with even a cathedral sitting silently in his shadow. As for the wedding, allow me to go into detail because I was there, in a three-piece suit with a watch in my fob pocket. Téti-yette was decked out in lace and brilliants, while her husband wore exactly the same. The orchestra was not from the savannas, but from a far-off city where music was made only with violins and mandolins, contrabasses and harmonicas, and a heap of scrap iron with valves and slides. They launched into pastourelles, sonatas, interminable canzones, fandangos, fugues, rhapsodies, and cavatinas, which the guests withered with their scorn. The orchestra then trotted out quadrilles, high-steps, ill-bred beguines, torrid calypso, and toward the end, even some sensual calendas and exuberant vidés. Oh, things began to jump! And there was no skimping on the good cheer: they served all kinds of meats in all kinds of sauces with all kinds of vegetables. Even the rain would have been disgusted to see how freely the coconut rum punch was flowing. I didn't drink too much, but I drank plenty, thank you, and quite properly, too.

Dawn revealed a desolation of drunkards in sweaty quest of *café-salé*, the salty coffee that settles queasy stomachs. The mama was nestling deep in the chair where happiness is savored. The two oldest brothers were rallying their joie de vivre by cleaning out the ice-cream freezers. And the ugly boy was at the gate, anxiously squinting down the road where the newlyweds had discreetly disappeared. He had neither eaten nor drunk, nor even shaken a leg on the dance floor, but we all put that down to the endless account of his infirmities. He left the gate and sat before his imbecilic bushes, lost in the patient contemplation of their flowers.

Despite her love, Tétiyette had followed her husband with some uneasiness. She stole fleeting glances at his elegant self. Clippity-cloppity-clippity, the carriage horses galloped on and on. Helped by a good tailwind, they soon came to the peak of a mountain so high it poked buttons into the bellies of clouds. There stood a very fine figure of a house, with a view of the sea, and on all sides. Some deformed birds were soaring overhead. Cats raced along the endless eaves, striking fear into startled bats. The walls were overgrown with a parasitic plant called vermicelli. All was as beautiful and calm as the shadow cast by a presbytery at the death of its priest.

Tétiyette felt happy. This lasted for no more seconds than would fill a shot glass. Remarking that he was thirsty, her husband grabbed a couple of hens wandering loose beneath the veranda, and piercing their throats with a very long fingernail that had so far escaped notice, he quenched that thirst with the hot syrup of their death throes. Then he handed Tétiyette a bunch of keys and gave her the grand tour of the sugar works and all its mills. He had her climb eight staircases and walk along twenty corridors, where he pointed out the doors to her one by one: "You may open this one but not that one, you may open this one but not that one, you may," et cetera, "but not," et cetera. At these warnings, a chill came over Tétiyette. Finally her husband went down into the courtyard, and she watched as he called over a kind of rooster with a red beak, curling plumes, and the eyes of a performing dog. Scraping crumbs from a goat's horn with a knife, he fed the bird as he chanted:

Agoulame coquame volame
Agoulame coquame volame
Agoulame coquame volame

Not a song to hear on a midnight stroll, and it gave Tétiyette a definitive quiver of shivers. They say that even today, in her home behind a convent, she catches that song sneaking into her old-maid dreams. But back to our misfortune: the husband soon mounted an earless horse and vanished into the distance. Tétiyette found herself alone in the rustling, sighing house. Grubby silences passed through the halls and climbed the stairs. An anguish clung to the curtains, and sorrow lay every-where, everywhere, like a fine coating of dust. Holding the bundle of keys, she mechanically opened a few doors, and a few more, and then and there was seized with a frenzy heedless of all prohibition. Click-clack, click-clack, she opened and went on opening, discovering glacial gloom, old furniture writhing with roots from the pri-mordial tree, shapeless heaps smelling vaguely of dead jellyfish, shards of shattered cities, stacks of tibias hol-lowed into flutes, cemetery walls crawling with life. In one chamber she found whole heads of women's hair, swaying limply at the end of their ropes, while the shad-ows of another room revealed a profusion of glances without pupils or eyelids. One door opened onto glass jars boiling with tears. The next one revealed the wisdom tooth I lost along with my milk teeth—a horrible sight!

Realizing she was in the house of the Devil, Tétiyette shrieked: "Mama!" At her cry, the strange rooster exploded with cock-a-doodle-doos of alarm, his wings beating evil spells clear across the courtyard. The Devil (because if it wasn't him, it was one of that ilk) turned back, and to speed things along, from below his shoulder-blades he unfurled cobwebby wings, rackety with unceasing flappity-flaps. Sailing over bluffs and ravines, he soon alighted in front of Tétiyette, who was beginning to find this marriage annoying. "You disobeyed me!" snapped the Devil, and carried her off to a stifling red room, where he undressed her on a canopy bed wider than it was long and, without even admiring her beauty (the obsession of my dreams), he took off his own clothes, exposing to the livid light his hairs and scales and even his beastly and infernal turgescences. What happened next was gruesome: licking his chops, he sprinkled her with salt, pepper, aromatic spices, and a bit of oil he produced from a drawer in the bedside table. Then he explained to her (but she'd probably already guessed): "I'm going to eat you!" And Tétiyette screamed, "*Ti frè!*," "Lil' brother!" "*Ti frè!*"

At the other end of the country, as the ugly boy watched, the flowers on his ridiculous bushes wilted—bang!—like that. "*Sésé mwen ka débatt!*" he exclaimed. "My sister is in danger!" Taking this outburst for one of his follies, his mother called from between her slumberous sheets to request peace and quiet. He tried to awaken his brothers: "Our sister's in danger, our sister's in pain!" And he wept as he never had from any illness. But his brothers would not desert their dreams.

With no one to count on but himself, the ugly boy fetched a rubber band, collected a handful of copper coins so old they were worthless, and set out, taking tiny club-foot steps with his twisted legs. He teeter-tottered along until he stole the first horse he saw, then he galloped as swiftly as smoke, guided by his sister's suffering through whirling highways and byways. The mountain peak appeared, then the house on the peak, then the maleficent rooster before the house. The bird flew at him in a fury of beak and wings, but the ugly boy's hide was thick, and he sent the creature spinning with a light backhand. Thus released from enchantment, the rooster resumed its original form: a pustulous toad (and proud of it). The ugly boy entered the house, opened first one door and then another in this labyrinth, and he had lost his way when his big sister gave a cry of agony that helped him find it. Too weak to leap up the stairs in a single bound, he climbed them twenty at a time, quickly reaching the accursed room.

The Devil was coiled up in the sheets, his stomach suitably swollen by Tétiyette's flesh. The ugly boy twanged his rubber band and pierced the Devil's forehead with a copper coin, then used the sharp edge of another, worn wafer-thin, to slice open his belly. He pulled out Tétiyette, who was beside herself with the worst of all possible fears. The Devil stank like fifty dead cats. His corpse sank into the bed, which sank into the house, which sank into the earth. The brother and sister jumped out the front door just as a maw of bedrock swallowed down the whole affair. A big thorn tree sprang up on the spot, flap! Tétiyette embraced the cripple, who was from that moment on the most beloved of little brothers ever to play around my hut in the small hours of a sunny night. There—now you know!

Glan-Glan,
the Spat-Out Bird

Caché oiseau craché
oiseau frère du soleil

[Hidden bird spat out
bird brother of the sun]

— AIMÉ CÉSAIRE

When
Good
Friday
rolls around, and it's time for
the afternoon church service,
you can
hear
prayers
and
adorations
of the
cross on
all sides.

Me, I stay home on my best behavior, eating fritters and
drinking plain water. That's only prudent, my friend,
because they say that on Good Friday our unlucky land
is visited by things not of this world. As proof, I give
you the legend of a fine fellow, a man so sweet you
would have thought he was made of pastry cream. But
wisdom has it that good dogs don't find good bones.
Because of this (perhaps), our man did not come up
with a prize bone when he picked out his fiancée: a
woman in whose heart there was no room for pity, or
love, or the tiniest bit of tenderness; a woman who was
as mean—oh my!—as a seven-year case of mange. She
pushed this simple fellow around the way you goad a
mule, with a big stick or a swift kick. The husband's soul
was as bruised as the back of a beast of burden.

So: The wife woke up one Good Friday with a longing for a nice dish of game, and she nagged the poor man to go hunting. He held out all day long, but at the hour when hens fly to their perches above the shadows, he had to shoulder his chassepot and dash off into the woods, pursued by the scolding of his peppery spouse. Through the woods he walked along, walk-walk-walked, and walked along some more, peering gimlet-eyed into the brush and branches where game loves to lurk. But not a thing did he see, not a single thrush, not one sarcelle, not even the wing of a sunbird. Nothing but flies and mosquitos frequented his path. A thousand times he considered turning back to his hut, but the mere thought of his wife drove him on. Soon he came to the back end of the forest, where the trees were so old they weren't trees anymore. And that is the very place where he saw the bird. A bird that no hunter had yet named, the color of dark fire in the flickering twilight. A kind of feathered enchantment, swaying in a way birds just never do. Allow me to offer my opinion: I would have tiptoed away from such a sight, because when it comes to marvels, unless they're in a fairy tale, I keep my head down. However, our fellow leveled his chassepot at this lunar apparition. Then (which doesn't surprise me) the bird began to sing:

> *Take good aim, my lil' son*
> *Tililiton tililiton*
> *Yon Glan-Glan!*

Our man almost bolted, of course, but the image of his wife rooted him to the spot. Decidedly deranged, he clambered up the tree to the branch where his prey sat, and when he reached for it, the bird whistled:

> *Hold me tight, my lil' son*
> *Tililiton tililiton*
> *Yon Glan-Glan!*

He grabbed the docile creature, pinioned it with slender vines, and returned to his hut, as proud as any hunter after a fearsome slaughter. Showing his wondrous find to his wife, he whined, "*Noupa pé valé on bèt konsa!*" "We can't eat a creature like this!" But his wife was wicked. Perhaps she was afraid of change; in any case, wicked she remained. Snatching up the bird, she wrung its neck, plucked it, gutted it, and chopped it into pieces, ummoved by the cooing that foamed from its beak:

> *Kill me well, my lil' daughter*
> *Tililiton tililiton*
> *Yon Glan-Glan!*

Soon the hut was filled with the fragrance of fricassee. The sputtering of onions. The scent of seven spices. The aroma of peppers. Some say she even prepared a codfish stew and some lovely smoked herrings besides, as well as a dish of salt meat in a tangy sauce. This was what the old folks call a good feed. The poor husband didn't have the heart to taste a morsel of it. All he could think about was the creature's charms, and its mysterious songs. He took a swallow of spirits, and a bite of a fritter, and that's how he spent the evening while his wife feasted royally. She ate everything, sucking on the bones, licking up the gravy, scraping the pot bottoms, and only the odd belch of pleasure stayed the grinding of her teeth. "*Ité dous!*" she exclaimed. "That was tasty!" Her husband sat as if entranced, his eyes veiled by flights of dazzling birds, his eyelids fluttering like great wings. Sometimes, a red mist floated in his head, and he dozed amid flocking dreams of feathers.

Hoisting him up by his armpits, his wife led him off to their bedroom, where (by the light of a little flame burning—eternally—in honor of some sanctified white man) she plunged into one of those deep sleeps that refresh neither body nor soul. Her husband tossed and turned, drowsing fitfully. Round about midnight, the wife felt her stomach begin to churn. In a dream, she saw herself inhabited by huge ferns, then by sinister mosses that piled up into cities, all to the accompaniment of waterfalling gurgles, rumbling gargles, and swirling bubbles. She started awake when a voice called to her from throughout her entire body:

> *Spit me out, my lil' daughter*
> *Tililiton tililiton*
> *Yon Glan-Glan!*

"*Ankay pwan an sirin,*" thought the woman. "I need some fresh air." Sitting in the rocking chair, watched by the moon, the woman felt herself growing dizzy, while the voice shook her very bones. The good-natured husband searched anxiously through the garden for a medicinal herb. He could hear his wife groaning, and then he heard her rush to a pot inside the hut to throw up her supper. She took a deep breath of relief. Her husband embraced her. They were about to return to their pallet when the spat-out supper began calling to them:

> *Stick me back together, my lil' daughter*
> *Tililiton tililiton*
> *Yon Glan-Glan!*

The sepulchral voice reverberated inside the pot. I can't say it took them long to get busy (it wouldn't have taken that much to get *my* full attention). They slaved the night away, sifting through the slop, tying up the fibers, jamming bits of bone together, reconstructing the beak, or the curve of an eyelid. Oh, puzzle beyond measure! Oh, wretched mess! They experienced the weariness that follows dire fatigue. The bird put on flesh, took shape, and finally, they held its quivering body in their accursed fingers. Then they jumped back, intending to race off to sanctuary in a church, but the lordly voice rang out again:

> *Put my feathers back, my lil' daughter*
> *Tililiton tililiton*
> *Yon Glan-Glan!*

They must have made quite a sight, looking right and left and here and there for the bird's plumage! The large quills were the easiest to find. The remiges lay beneath long rainbows. The rectrices glimmered with phosphorescence in the dark. But as they sought the filoplumes and the vibrissae, the hut became vast, and their yard became the world. They went through seven cases of candles lighting up each speck of the floor, the walls, the ceiling. They crawled on all fours, ploughing up the dust with their noses. They spent the next day like that, and part of the following night. Then the bird stood again in all its former splendor, glaring at them with a cold and angry eye. It flapped one wing, then the other, and finally poked about beneath them with its beak. The poor fellow and his wife lay prostrate with nausea and distress, their ordeal at an end, they thought.... But the bird began to sway, and sang out one more time:

> *I'm missing a feather, my lil' daughter*
> *Tililiton tililiton*
> *Yon Glan-Glan!*

And they searched for this last bit of down, their souls in ashes from exhaustion. They carried the furniture outside. They took it all apart, piece by piece. They peeled off the newspaper covering the walls. They explored between the planks, ripping them apart one by one. Then they took off the roof, and demolished the hut, reducing it to rubble. They found the fluffy feather snagged on a beam. The bird tallied up its plumes and away it flew, the way dreams do.

They say that after this, the shrewish wife became a loving and kind woman, and even a vegetarian, so that the poor husband grew tired of this happiness and married someone else. But that's his business! Me, on Good Friday, I stay home on my best behavior.

Yé, Master of Famine

Here is the story of
Yé,
a tale once told

to Lafcadio Hearn.

Oh, Yé, he was really
one bad man,
all made of faults.

A malingerer, he shied away from any labor in the Békés' fields or in their sugar works, refusing to toil even in their mills. He hated the starvation that dogged his idle heels, and he skulked all over with wide-open mouth, a bottomless pit looking to take a taste or a bite wherever he could. His wretched wife had the heart of a sheep: a meek creature and no mistake. These two had brought into misery a slew of children, and the whole lot of them spent every day that the Goodlord made braiding the bitter vines of hunger. More than one overseer tried to recruit them to cut sugar cane, or cart this harvest to the works, or do I-don't-know-what other delightful chore that sucks the life out of the poor folks in this land. But Yé, that dog, he loved his freedom. His wife and children loved theirs even more. In spite of their misfortune, they held their heads up high and kept an eye out for what the future might bring. Alas! Yé was under a curse, the result of a nasty quarrel with the deathwatch beetles in the days when the latter would traipse through copses in great processions, lustily chanting this song:

Baron, baron, tonton tolomba lomba
Azon zon zon: ba li koté kian kian kian

The deathwatches were good creatures. They never tortured anyone and hated to see suffering. And so, because they knew how little inclined they were to share, they never invited guests to the feasts they held every year beneath the light of a full moon. A child at the time, and already voracious, Yé followed them. Crouching beneath the leaves, he accompanied their procession to the backwoods, where the woods give way to more woods. In the distance, Yé could see the clearing where the feast was to be held, and as the beetles were none too speedy, he strode off smartly and arrived before them. While the procession wound its way around roots, mosses, and mushrooms, Yé devoured the entire banquet, singing their song:

Baron, baron, tonton tolomba lomba
Azon zon zon: ba li koté kian kian kian

Now, deathwatches never trifle when it comes to food. Seeing there was nothing left to eat but wood (and in fact, that's all they've lived on ever since), they lifted up their twenty-seven thousand rumps as one and let out a unanimous curse, of the kind that take their time but never miss. In spite of their awesome anger and their sour bellies full of dry sawdust, the death-watches set out once more in their slow procession, beetling along with tiny steps and singing in tiny voices:

Baron, baron, tonton tolomba lomba
Azon zon zon: ba li koté kian kian kian

Of course, time passed, and the curse (a keen-nosed bitch he had no chance of shaking off) followed Yé to pounce upon him in the prime of his life. Here's how it happened. As he did each day, our man was prowling through the underbrush in search of the odd stray hen, sleeping manicou, or yam out for a stroll. In short, he was looking for a chance to use his teeth to fill his tummy. He heard: "Tak! Tak! Tak tak tak!" Then he heard it again: "Tak tikitak tak!" Small explosions, or else pretty big farts. Peering up ahead, he could make out in the center of a clearing a kind of indescribable being made of leather, flabby flesh, and gleaming mahogany. Sitting before a fire, the thing was roasting a batch of snails, whose shells were snapping in the flames like a string of firecrackers.

Yé rubbed his eyes and still saw the same thing. This thing, which was as thick as a breadfruit tree, had a vaguely human aspect as it sat there blissfully wolfing down impressive handfuls of crispy little bodies. Which smelled appetizing. Hardly to his surprise, Yé found his lips oily with famished longing. Sharpening his gaze, he saw that the thing had no eyelids or even any eyeballs. He approached the unbelievable sight: roasted snails, splashed with a peppery sauce, lay strewn upon a tongue that gobbled them up flip-flap! Without paying any attention to those huge nostrils, quivering as they sniffed up smells (including his own, naturally), Yé reached out over the coals and helped himself to one snail, then another, and another. With his well-trained teeth, he was soon eating as fast and as much as the thing. Finally they were down to the last shell. Yé meant to grab it and run, but he was seized by the collar in a vise-like grip. "'Od's blood!" shouted the thing. "I've got you—you're mine!" Without more ado, it perched itself on Yé's shoulders. "Take me home with you," it commanded him.

There are days when just nothing goes right. When his wife and children first caught sight of Yé in the distance, they thought he was toting home a fine quarter of beef. Dispensing with music, they danced in premature delight, and their teeth gleamed with the dew of constant hunger. A closer look sent them scurrying for cover. The children hid beneath the mattresses, in a string's shadow, behind spider webs (oh, when you're thin, it's so easy to hide!). As for the mama, she slipped behind the door like a broomstick. The thing curled up in a corner of their hovel and stayed there, except on the rare occasions when there was something to eat. The Yé family wasted away and even farther. If our man brought home an ortolan's wing, a kid's tail, a dry crust, a shriveled potato, or a yellowed breadfruit, the thing—as though it were asleep—would let them sit down around the table and serve up the windfall on their little plates, but before they could ply their forks, it would blow a magic breath that left the family bewitched, unconscious, paralyzed. Then the thing would climb onto the table, slurp up their pathetic meal, and relieve itself on each plate. Awakening its victims, it would shout, "Lick those plates clean!" And they would! Oh, it brings tears to my eyes.

This went on throughout the tangerine season and the sweetsop season as well. Yé, his wife, and their brood showed all the signs of ill health: pimples, bruises, bald spots. They slept poorly, because at night the thing's snoring shook the hovel and rattled the nails out of the roof. One day the mama couldn't take this anymore. "*Ay wê Bondié, mandé'y an pawol,*" she told Yé. "Go see the Goodlord and ask his advice." In those days of yesteryear, the Goodlord was only a country policeman off in a backwater. He had not yet assumed all his divine powers and lived modestly among us, spending his Sundays in a hut of spun stars set in the thickest of thickets.

Early one Sunday, Yé set out to meet him there. He strode smartly along and reached a gray mist full of silence floating upon a layer of steely blue. In the center, amid the trunks of luminous trees, he glimpsed the lunar hut. Before he could open his mouth, the Goodlord announced (from everywhere and nowhere): "*Anja sav sa ou lé.*" "I already know what you want." And he told Yé that the thing was a devil, that Yé had to return home without eating anything along the way, that he had to prepare a meal there, and that when the devil rose up, Yé was to shout:

> *Tam ni pou tam ni bè*
> *Tam ni pou tam ni bè!*

That would drop the devil down dead, God willing.
Yé repeated that sacred charm as he trudged along:
"*Tam ni pou tam ni bè, tam ni pou tam ni bè…*" His old
friend famine soon stopped him beneath a few clusters
of guavas, near some greengages and coco plums that
he devoured without a second thought. And all the way
back, our man gummed up his teeth—and his memory—with whatever junk he could find. Arriving home
with a handful of crawdads from the river, he demanded
confidently that they be fried up without delay. When
everyone was served, the Devil (because if it wasn't him,
it was another just like him) stood up the way he always
did. He was about to blow on them all when Yé cried
out arrogantly:

Ann toké dyab la kagnan!

Which, of course, had not the slightest effect. The
Devil blew on them, devoured their crawdads, and awakened them to eat his excrement. Then he curled up for a
quiet nap in the corner of the hut—oh, I can feel those
tears welling up in my eyes! Seven times, yes, seven times
Yé went off to the Goodlord's place, listened to the
charm, lost it along the way by gorging himself on fruits,
and ended up screaming nonsense at the Devil at the cru-
cial moment. The mama made the face of despair and
pulled out her hair. The children were permanently sunk
in a sniveling sadness. Luckily, in this raft of children,
there was a littlest one, not as thin as the others because
he was slyer than a rat. Ti-fonté, they called him. He was
insolent and afraid of nothing, not even the Devil
(although he had never attacked him, which proved he

was clever indeed). Seeing his mama's distress, he said, "*Kité'm désann dèhiè Papa, é manké mitanné sa.*" "Let me follow Papa, and I'll take care of this." His mama knew how cunning he was, and gave her consent. Yé, thank goodness, always wore—rain or shine, day or night—a flowing coat called a lavalasse, equipped with large buttons and pockets as big as *that,* which he loaded up with the spoils of his wanderings. Gloof! Ti-fonté slipped into one of them just before Yé set out, and when his papa stood before the Goodlord, the child made sure he didn't miss a word. The Goodlord chewed Yé out something fierce (in those days, he still lost his temper), then slowly, carefully, he re-peat-ed:

> *Tam ni pou tam ni bè*
> *Tam ni pou tam ni bè!*

Ti-fonté heard everything, and clearly, too. He wrapped those words up in his entire brain, and sealed them fast with a good dollop of memory. He moistened his tongue so that the words would ring out nicely. The idea that their ordeal might soon be over sent tears of joy to refresh his eyes. As for Yé, out of sheer habit he gathered this, he plucked that, taking note along the way of a promising yam leaf, estimating the maturity of a distant cluster of fruit, marking trunks with signs visible only to himself—in short, exercising that art of survival taught to him by his friend famine. Back home, Ti-fonté sprang quick-quick from that pocket. "*Bagay là obidjoul!*" he told his mama. "All's well!" Meanwhile, Yé pulled from his other pockets three blue crabs and a breadfruit, which—given the circumstances—was rich fare indeed.

Everything was cooked, everyone was served. Then the Devil made his move, and Yé began to shout:

Ann toké dyab la kagnan!

Ti-fonté stood up too and screamed:

Tam ni pou tam ni bè
Tam ni pou tam ni bè!

You would have thought the Devil had been beaned by a coconut. He was transfixed, seized with convulsions, foaming at the mouth. They watched him stagger about in a bad way, rumbling like a volcano, and then fall stiff, dead, and already cold. Oh, no more tears! The Yé family ate their meal as they capered around the body, which soon swelled and began to stink. Tying a rope to a protuberance, they dragged the corpse out onto the heap of rocks Yé called his garden. (In spite of all his efforts, he had never managed to grow anything whatsoever.) Out there in the sun, the Devil's body turned blue, then banana-purple, then proceeded to ooze reptilian odors. Soon it exploded, scattering itself all over the rocky soil which then and there, like all the Devil's chamberpots, became exceedingly fertile. The entire region became a blessed garden called Grosmorne, where one had only to think of a fruit to see it appear upon a bough. I tell you that quite on his own, Yé recovered his taste for work and forgot all about famine, whereas I myself, driven from the sugar mills when the cane ran out, had to go learn from him how to outwit hunger. Oh, life is funny sometimes....

The Accra of Riches

An old woman

lay despairing on her deathbed;

despite wasting her youth in the cane fields, she had nothing to leave her son except one of those little fritters called accras. "If only it were hot, at least!" she said, and died. And it's true: a piping hot accra is tastier, so it's worth more. Her son (named Ti-zèb) waked her, buried her, had a mass said for her, and set out on his travels. He took along his stale accra, nicely wrapped in a banana leaf. He walked along, double-time, triple-time, taking smaller steps so he could take more of them, so eager was he to be wind ahead. When he felt hungry, he spared the accra by picking a guava.

He soon came in sight of a house as tall as a thirty-year-old tree, where he knocked on the door to request a bed for the night and received a gracious welcome. Then Ti-zèb announced that his accra would sleep only in a hen house. Astonishment and upset all around: the chickens would surely eat it, the turkeys would make short work of it.... Their guest reassured them: the accra was stale, as hard as an ancient bread heel, so no beak would risk pecking it. "*Sé labitid li, pon poul ké modey,*" he said. "It's used to this, the hens won't bother it." So the accra was installed in the center of the hen house. Everyone, and Ti-zèb, went off to bed.

Later that night, our boy sneaked into the hen house and ate the accra with relish, quite pleased that none of the chickens had snapped up his mother's last posses-sion. At dawn, he began to wail:

> *My accra, my accra!*
> *Ti lanni yo! Ti lanni!*

Everyone started awake: Wha? Wha? Ti-zèb put on quite a circus, crying rivers and snatching out tufts of his hair. Those confounded birds had eaten his accra! And such a nice one, too! He'd go complain to the police if he wasn't given a fine rooster to make good his loss! His hosts (being less than fond of your full-blown low-life tantrum) preferred to put a quick end to this sordid affair: they gave him a rooster with a violet comb and an elegant tail.

With his prize under his arm, Ti-zèb went on his way, and going this way and that way, he made his way come nightfall to another house, as tall as a fifty-year-old tree and surrounded by fenced-in fields of grazing sheep. Ti-zèb asked for a bed and a little spot for his rooster in the flock of sheep. Amazement, misgivings: "*Mouton la ké krasé'y,*" "The sheep will trample it." Ti-zèb replied that his rooster slept that way all the time, perched on a sheep's back. So the bird was set down among the beasts, and everyone went off to bed. Later that night, Ti-zèb slipped out to the rooster, cracked its ribs, and wrung its neck. At dawn, he swept away the last sluggish drops of tender slumber with bloodcurdling screams:

> *My rooster, my rooster!*
> *Ti lanni yo! Ti lanni!*

The entire household was treated to an up-close display of the utmost grief. Such a handsome bird! Squashed by a ram! Undoubtedly a most ferocious ram! And blah blah blah....These people were not used to raised voices.

Shaken by all this commotion, they offered a ram as feeble compensation. Despite eyes blurred with tears, Ti-zèb managed to select the biggest animal. He slipped a rope around its neck and set off, weeping, down the dusty road.

By highroads and byroads and side roads he went, until he arrived that night at a large house, as tall as a sixty-year-old tree, surrounded by a fenced-in pasture where cattle lay chewing their cuds. He requested a bed, and then asked if his ram might pass the night, as was its custom, with its friends, the cattle. This was arranged. All went to sleep. Later that night, Ti-zèb stole out to the ram, broke its neck, and fell to wailing at sunrise:

My ram, my ram!
Ti lanni yo! Ti lanni!

Those in the house thought all hell was at their door. Such a splendid ram! Crushed by an ox! And blah blah blah....To placate Ti-zèb, they spontaneously offered him an ox, a prime animal, black and white with nice thick hoofs. Their guest needed no persuasion, and moaning pitifully, he led the animal away.

Ladies and gentlemen, allow me a chuckle here, because the last deal is the best of the lot! That afternoon, ambling along with his ox, he ran into two fellows transporting a coffin. The dear departed was a little mulatto who had died of grief at having a black woman for a mother. Ti-zèb suggested a swap: the corpse for the ox. The two carters had no mulattoes in their families, so they blithely opened the coffin, gave him the body, and replaced the lid over a load of stones. Overjoyed with their ox, they danced off.

❧ 89 ❧

Ti-zèb hid in a canebrake to avoid being seen lugging a dead man. At dusk he made his way to a great house, as tall as a hundred-year-old tree, with ten thousand windows, fifty thousand rooms, and thirty-six lightning rods. It was the mansion of a rich man, whose only treasures, however (at least in his eyes), were his two or three daughters of marriageable age. Ti-zèb asked for lodging for himself and his brother, who was already fast asleep across his shoulders. The body was put to bed in one room, and Ti-zèb was given another. After feasting on papaya au gratin and zabitan soup, everyone went off to pick sweet dreams. At dawn, Ti-zèb dashed into his "brother's" room and shattered the peace of dreamland with screams of anguish:

My brother has been killed!
Ti lanni yo! Ti lanni!

The ladies and gentlemen felt as though they had awakened in a fishmarket. Ti-zèb raked his face with his fingernails, threw himself upon the body, dashed to the window to shriek of his distress. Soon the rabble came pouring from their nearby huts, all eyes on Ti-zèb, and two mounted policemen showed up, straining their official ears to catch every word. The rich man (who had never—in all his life!—imagined that a throat could utter such cries) raised his hands in a gesture of appeasement. "I will make amends," he promised. "What would you like?" Oh, what do you think Ti-zèb asked for: the house, or one of the daughters in marriage? In any case, me, when I go traveling, I always carry an accra tucked snugly in my pocket.

Ti-Jean Horizon

Poverty is a breeding ground for intelligence and guile.

Here is the first exploit of the wiliest little fellow ever to survive in the Békés' fields. One of these white folks had refused (as usual) to acknowledge the child he had fathered on his servant. Instead, he became the boy's godfather: a fancy way of washing his hands of him. Now this child, ladies and gentlemen, was named Ti-Jean, a name that would become a symbol of relentless mischief, the very incarnation of naughtiness. The misery in which his mother and fifteen brothers and sisters lived was something cruel. Ti-Jean, a sensitive and vindictive soul, resolved to make a fool of his godfather and steal all his money, if this was at all possible. It was. Here's the how of it.

He got his godfather to take him on as a kind of handy boy, handy for better or for worse. Once installed in the Béké's shadow, Ti-Jean bided his time. Which came on the occasion of a party that the Béké could not postpone, even though his cook was confined to her bed with a difficult pregnancy. "*Manjé mwen sé mwen menm,*" announced

Ti-Jean. "Cooking is my specialty." His godfather left him in charge of everything: hunting the manicous, seasoning them just right; slaughtering chickens, sheep, ducks, and game; preparing the meats and pâtés; cleaning the offal; picking the herbs and spices, chopping and grating them; and popping all this into fifteen stewpots over a nice spread of glowing charcoal. Hubble-bubble, the pots were boiling hard. The guests waited, enjoying the punches and the savory fritters. Their nostrils flared, tantalized by delightful aromas. Soon their bellies began to bite them, and they asked if the food was going to spend the day in the kitchen. Their host went off laughing to see how things were coming along.

A strange sight greeted him: the fire was out, and the pots were sitting on the floor, bubbling away beneath the crack of Ti-Jean's whip. He had removed them from the coals only a moment before, and now he persuaded his godfather that they were boiling by the heat of his whip. "Cook, cook, cook away," he sang to the pots, snapping his whip. Not a man known for his sparkling intellect, the godfather said to himself, "But this is a magic whip!" He demanded that Ti-Jean sell it to him. The boy protested, "*Parin ô, fwèt tala ké poté'w dévenn!*" "Oh, Godfather, this whip will bring you nothing but trouble!" Instead of paying him heed, the white man paid Ti-Jean the first—and certainly not the last—money he ever received in his life, stashed the whip away, and went off to celebrate with his fellow Békés. Over desert he exclaimed, "Gentlemen, this was good, but next Sunday, on the Feast of Saint Peter, it will be better. Don't make any other plans, because the best eating anywhere will be right here!" He was thinking, of course, of his marvelous whip.

All the guests accepted his invitation and returned the following Sunday, as famished as hunchbacks with growing humps to feed. The skin over their bellies was sticking to the skin on their backs, because they'd been fasting in preparation for the banquet. Their wives and children had come along too, eager for the promised treats. Ti-Jean, laid low by a case of make-believe flu, spent the day hiding out in his hut. The guests drank their tafias and fruit juices out on the veranda and sank their teeth into the pickled appetizers, but they soon noticed that the refreshing breeze was disconcertingly free of cooking aromas. Nothing. Not one breath of simmering stew, not one sigh from a crackling fricassee. They began mouthing off, pounding on the table, bellowing with anger. Out in the kitchen, sweating like a hangman at confession, their host (who had hunted and chopped and seasoned everything himself) was whipping the huge pots in vain, flogging them left and right, and singing the song Ti-Jean had sung:

Canaris bouilli bouilli bouilli
Canaris bouilli bouilli bouilli

But not one sauce would thicken. The fats and oils stayed greasy-cold. The meat stubbornly refused to brown. "Ti-Jean played a trick on me," he explained to his guests, who were steaming red with hunger and rage, and in no mood for excuses. They tipped over the stewpans, broke the chairs, and swatted their host with hats and gloves. Since they were people of a most ill-mannered sort, they pissed on the tablecloths and did things in the potted plants. Ti-Jean's godfather came looking for him in shreds and tatters, clutching a pistol.

All his brothers and sisters were out in the fields, so Ti-Jean was home alone with his mother. After long and anxious thought, he had come up with a scheme: a bullock's bladder stuffed with chicken guts and other disgusting sundries, which he asked his old mother to wear under her apron. He also told her to play dead when he cut open the bladder with a single knife thrust, and not to move until she heard him play his flute and bid her rise. With the stage thus set, he plunged into the deepest of sleeps, the one that is just pretend.

The godfather burst in, sputtering showers of abuse and shouting for Ti-Jean. "But he's sleeping!" protested the mama. "Then wake him up!" squawked the godfather. "*Iké tchimen*," warned the mama. "He'll be furious!" Then she shook Ti-Jean, who leaped up from his fictitious nap in an even more fictitious rage. Grabbing the waiting knife, he slit open her belly. "*Man rayi yo lévé mwen*," he shrieked. "I hate to be awakened like that!" The poor woman fell down splat! And lay there festooned with bloody entrails.

Stunned, the godfather stammered, "You wretch, you've killed your mother!" "*Apa ayin*," sighed Ti-Jean. "It's nothing." Reaching for his little flute, he began to play:

> *Toutoutou toutoutou*
> *anlè jamb*

And the mama wriggled her legs.

> *Toutoutou toutoutou*
> *anlè bwa*

And the mama wiggled her arms.

> *Toutoutou toutoutou*
> *tout douboutt*

And the mama stood her whole self up. The godfather was quite flabberdegasky. He turned somewhat green, and somewhat blue, and then he begged Ti-Jean, "You have to sell me that flute!" Ti-Jean went through the entire routine, pretending to be much attached to the pipe, even predicting to his godfather that it would only bring him troubles, and much, much worse ones than he'd had with the whip. The Béké insisted. That's how Ti-Jean earned the second sum of money of his short little life.

While he was counting his coins, his godfather went home in great eagerness to try out this fabulous magic. He climbed up to the attic where he kept his old mother (a sort of yellowish gauze with a gray mane and colorless eyes), picked her up from her rocking chair, and stabbed her in the stomach. The yellowish gauze crumpled without a word, irreparably rumpled on the polished parquet. Wreathed in smiles, the Béké pulled out the flute to tootle:

> *Toutoutou toutoutou*
> *anlè jamb*

But the mama did not wriggle her legs.

> *Toutoutou toutoutou*
> *anlè bwa*

❦ 97 ❦

But the mama did not wiggle her arms.

Toutoutou toutoutou
tout douboutt

But the mama remained more buggered up than an arrogantly tall filao tree with its drooping branches all snarled by the wind. The Béké tried again and so on, for six long days. When the lunar gauze became a whitish sludge, he realized that he had killed his mother and began to scream the thirteen sorrows of the world. People came from miles around to contemplate this tragedy. Freedmen, field slaves, mulattoes in gaudy vests, hardscrabble Békés and well-to-do Békés, many kinds of mounted policemen—all listened to the story of Ti-Jean's malicious trick.

"What a little devil!" they said. "He's a snake! A sorcerer! We should stuff him in a bag and throw it into the sea, way off by the horizon...." (Oh, the story's title is now becoming clear!) They set out with great pomp and a great sack. Surrounding the hut, invading through doors and windows, they laid hands on Ti-Jean, stuck him headfirst into the gaping bag, secured it with some mahoe twine, and swarmed off toward the sea. Luckily for our boy, their route took them past a new distillery, where a young Béké was trying to create something novel in the rum line. Everyone felt suddenly thirsty and wanted a taste, so they left the sack in the grass by the roadside and vanished into the vapor of the huge casks.

Ti-Jean was crying wah-wah-wah when he heard the limping step of an old man of rheumatic age. Now he began weeping and wailing and moaning and groaning that they were going to drown him on the horizon because of an ox he had been set to watch that had trampled a Béké's seed bed.... The old man was much moved, and thought, well hell, a little boy's life was worth more than some mess of seedlings, so he opened up the bag. Ti-Jean sprang out like a fountain, hugged his rescuer, and got busy cramming the trunk of a withered banana tree into the bag. Then, peeping out from a ravine, he awaited the return of the avengers. These worthies had downed a fine snootful of rum. They hoisted the sack without noticing a thing and set off with uh-uh-uh-unsteady steps to fling it into the sea. Sploosh! As he watched them laughing while the sack was swept off to the horizon by wicked currents ("Ti-Jean Hori-zon! Ti-Jean Hori-zon!" they chanted), our boy began working on a way to finish with his Béké godfather once and for all.

He schemed, and schemed, and schemed, and as he was scheming, along came a large herd of horned beasts followed by an oh-so-rickety fellow who thought oh-so-highly of himself. Ti-Jean dazzled him with words and managed to borrow the herd for awhile. A little later, the godfather was enjoying the breeze out on his veranda while the gravediggers dug a hole for his mother. "Woo woo woo," he heard, and then seven hundred head of horned beasts trotted down the hillside before his very eyes, which he couldn't believe because right behind them came Ti-Jean, whistling like a teakettle. Making his way through the sea of horns, the Béké called to his godson, "Hey, is it you or not? Didn't I just drown you off on the horizon?"

"Hello there, Godfather, *an sôti lorizon*," said Ti-Jean.

"I've just returned from the horizon." The Béké wanted to know who owned such a handsome herd of animals. Ti-Jean explained that he'd brought them back with him and regretted not having been thrown even farther, because then he would have returned with twenty-two herds just like it. The horizon, he added (for the information of the stupefied Béké), was a field of meek and milling beasts, in great need of a master with a stick to guide them. He, Ti-Jean, couldn't wait to go back there. "Oh, my dear godson," whimpered the Béké, "take me to the horizon! A herd like that one is a treasure indeed!" And—before he had any chance to think it over—Ti-Jean clapped him into a sack, tied it with the same piece of mahoe twine, and weighted the whole thing with boulders. At the seashore he took a dinghy and row-row-rowed toward the horizon. The godfather asked impatiently, "Is it much farther?" When Ti-Jean stopped rowing, he grabbed the sack and mockingly advised his godfather to choose the choicest animals. Then, without even a one-two-three, he heaved him overboard. Ploop! The sack plummeted like a hunk of locust wood.

Ti-Jean went straight back to the Béké's house; called together all the field slaves, the white manager, the mulatto overseers; lined up the servants; and announced, "My godfather has gone off to France for a short while, and he asked me to keep my little eye on everything in the meantime." We believed him and we obeyed him, so that he became the acting heir apparent of someone fated to search forever on the horizon for invisible flocks, someone so lost by now that you couldn't even carve a trumpet from what's left of his bones.

Nanie-Rosette
the Belly-Slave

Ladies and gentlemen,

gluttony is no sin,

but don't tell me that,

because there was a time

when greediness had

a devil all its own,

who would

come prowling around

the hapless glutton

to stir up trouble.

In those days, greedy-guts would find themselves swallowed off the face of this earth into its bowels, into the very worst parts of hell. They say—just to show you what I mean—that a mother once gave birth to gluttony itself, and her name was Nanie-Rosette. Quite a pretty name for a disaster with an abyss for a stomach, a riverbed for a throat, and a kind of grinding mill where her mouth and teeth should have been. In short, Nanie-Rosette loved to eat, oh yes. She ate to eat, whether hungry or no. And when she really was hungry—let's not even talk about it, because no one could describe the voracity of her assault on stewpots, bunches of fruit, and sweets of all kinds. And, most heartrending of all, this food seemed to go entirely to waste: instead of being a plump dumpling, Nanie-Rosette was a scrawny little thing for her age, no fatter than the shadow of a grass blade. She was so thin that her mother, who often tried to beat this vice out of her, was always afraid she would break apart, and be lost. So after each shower of slaps, her mother showered her with candy to console her. While Nanie-Rosette ate, sucked, and licked, her mother worried or wept.

It was on the day of a christening party that the girl carried her greediness to extremes and somewhat beyond. Even before the hostess had removed the lids from her pots and pans, Nanie-Rosette had already claimed her share and that of ten other guests. The young lady was clutching a plate overflowing with Angola peas, breadfruit, codfish fritters, peppery octopus, crawfish cooked in a court-bouillon, avocado slices dusted with flour, and a heap of sweetmeats. She'd made a good haul, and now had to fend off all the other pestering brats sniffing hungrily around in the back of the kitchen. That's why she went outside, and then even farther, for she went into the woods, but still she couldn't find a good spot: over here were ants crying for a mouthful; over there, the flies and bees were begging for a taste; over that way was a cat; and just ahead, a dog. Nanie-Rosette soon reached the remotest part of the forest, where the trees seem like old women muttering in a twilight where no flowers grow.

In this place of unquiet eternity, Nanie-Rosette sat down contentedly on a rock, a great big rock, very nicely situated, too nicely situated, a rock that all the birds were careful to avoid. (And so was I.) Comfortably settled, Nanie-Rosette ate her fill and more. Not one creature of any kind approached her to ask for a bite. Life would have seemed simply wonderful if she hadn't felt thirsty and tried to go get a drink. That was when she discovered she was now *rooted* to the rock. Oh, a bad business indeed! Our young lady could go neither to the right nor to the left, neither up nor down, and since I don't want to pile on too much trouble, I won't mention the diagonals. She spent the rest of her day wriggling. When Master Sun began calling his sunbeams home, Nanie-Rosette did what we all do when we're scared silly: she screamed for her mama.

Luckily, she had one, a mama as strong as a staff that just won't break, no matter how hard you lean on it. "Mama!" wept Nanie-Rosette. Her mother was already scouring the woods, and when she heard the girl's cries, she hastened off in that direction. "*Roye, sé wôch dyab-la kila!*" she shrieked, when she came in sight of the great boulder. "Alas! That's the devil's rock!" While Nanie-Rosette stepped up the volume of her tears, the mama tried to tear her loose from this evil spell. She pulled. She lifted. She even tried to tip over the rock, and then the forest, and finally all the misery in the world. It was not despair that stopped her short, but the simple sliding of the sun toward a horizon in deep mourning. She had precious little time left, and had to act quickly.

"*Espéré mwen,* wait for me patiently," she whispered to her daughter. Back through the woods she went at a run and straight on into town, where in no time she rounded up thirty joiners, twelve unlicensed carpenters, one hundred and fifty-six nail-pounders, and an et cetera of apprentices who were quite conscientious in matters of iron fittings and fortifications. They all closed up shop, leaving their work up in the air (luckily, there was no wind that day), and followed the mama back into the forest. They were a peculiar bunch, and their eyes had that dreamy look you see in people who don't talk much. As soon as they laid those eyes on Nanie-Rosette, still stuck fast to her rock, they opened secret compartments in the bottoms of their toolboxes and brought out handsaws forged by the light of a full moon, bone-handled hammers with silver heads, pins, bolts, and tacks to be touched only with the left hand. They unpacked long-shafted mortising axes that shone with an inner force, giant chisels, adzes the likes of which had never been seen in those parts, tracing awls, rulers, pencils, augers engraved with mystic signs. Then, walking in crooked lines, they sought out strange trees whose reddish bark, when opened in a cross-shaped cut, revealed a store of planks and beams, battens and posts, which they carried jauntily away, whistling prayers all the while.

And now, in a race with nightfall, a hut began to rise around Nanie-Rosette. The magical tools worked silently, guided by the experienced hands of the carpenters, who kept a constant eye on the setting sun. Nanie-Rosette sat inside a framework that enclosed a good part of the rock before enveloping her within an impossible structure. It was put together every which way, with tongue-and-groove joints, joggles, scarf joints, and dovetails that forced the wooden pieces into seamless unity. And yet the iron fittings were laid on with a lavish hand, so that the fiery sunset blazed upon a seemingly impregnable array of metal flanges, rivets, brackets, and plates. Before the last light died away in a pall of mortuary violet, the walls and roof of this fortlet were in place. Next came a door as thick as an ox's back, which the iron-smiths secured with thirteen hinges, thirteen flat bolts, thirteen sliding bolts, and a truly formidable deadlock.

"*Ma fi, pas fè betiz,*" Nanie-Rosette's mama warned her daughter as she gave her the key. "Don't do anything foolish!" She also told her not to open the door to anyone, except when the voice of her very own mama sang out to her. Anxious at the gathering gloom, the carpenters dragged this most reluctant lady far away from that nasty old rock. It belonged—you guessed it—to the devil of gluttony, and was a place where werewolves, ghouls, and winged wraiths gather to carouse the night away, devouring things fried in snake fat and swilling murky water scooped up from cemetery puddles. Such refreshments made the revelers shimmer on moonless nights, and for a few fleeting moments, these sad creatures imagined themselves to be the natural children of stars or fireflies.

On that particular night, they arrived with a terrific din of wing-flapping and hoof-clopping that set Nanie-Rosette a-tremble. She could hear them banging into the walls, one after another; she heard their cries of amusement and disbelief, and the scraping of their claws. They circled the hut, then landed heavily on the roof, which they trampled ferociously. Soon the air was filled with the horrific grunting of the devil of gluttony. He arrived bearing delicacies it would be best not to mention. His astonishment was expressed in hoots, in hisses, in the barking of chained dogs, as though different creatures were fighting it out in his throat. At times, he was silent. Then Nanie-Rosette could hear him breathing as he examined the joints of the hut, sputtering like a sick old cat, until a whiff of the girl's sugary smell wafting through a crack would set him braying again. This hellish company launched into a huge discussion. Torrents of abuse. Oaths. Tears. The sounds of shattered friendships, disappointed stomachs. The devil of gluttony would occasionally somersault over to lash the hut with his tail and skewer it with all his horns. Lumbering into the air, he would crash down upon the roof with infernal curses. Abandoned by his friends, he lingered, alone, at the foot of his desolate rock, gazing at it (I would imagine) with diabolical melancholy.

He was still there at dawn, crammed into the moldy shadow of a tree love-struck by lightning. At the song of the pippiree bird, the mama reappeared, escorted by friends and neighbors all agog with excitement. The carpenters began to niggle over their work, adding a board here, a bolt there, a little holy water any old where. Gathering around the rock, priests fell first to their knees and then to sleep, dreaming of prayers. Farther away, seancers and magicians skilled in counter-charms gestured majestically to unbind the spell. A crowd bearing crosses and rosaries ringed the spot with a circle of devotion. Standing before the door to the hut, the mama sang:

Nanie-Rosette mwen di'w
Nanie-Rosette dita Rosette dita Rosette
Sé mwen Nanie
Bagui di, bagui di, quin!
Sé mwen Nanie, dita Rosette

The first time she heard the song, Nanie-Rosette flipped the thirteen flat bolts. The second time, she pulled the thirteen sliding bolts. The third time, she undid the redoubtable deadlock and flung open the door. The mama kissed her; everyone kissed her. The mama gave her food; everyone gave her food. She ate with a brutal appetite while her hair was done in lovely braids. The day went by in advice and commiseration. One woman sang long-forgotten beguines to her. Another offered her dainty hand mirrors and perfumes from an English island. A man who had been to Europe told her of the fortunes and misfortunes of a girl named Cinderella. They tried and tried to free her from that rock, but at dusk they had to leave, dragging her mother away with them.

Lurking within spitting distance, his ears streaming in the breeze, the devil didn't miss a thing. He laughed up his sleeve, and down again for good measure. As the shadows lengthened, he sprang from his hiding place, cocksure of success. If he sang "*Nanie-Rosette mwen di'w*" once, he sang it a thousand times, but not a single bolt, pin, or lock on that hut so much as twitched. The devil of gluttony realized he had not picked quite the right moment, so he cooled his heels until just before dawn, when the mother wasn't due to return for some time yet. He sang "*Nanie-Rosette mwen di'w*" and repeated it seven thousand times. Not one flutter inside the hut. When the mama arrived and the door banged open at the sound of that mama-voice, the devil of gluttony realized that his voice was too thick, and too gross, too hoarse and skreaking, booming with cavernous echoes and the snap-crackling of an on-rushing forest fire. While everyone listened to Nanie-Rosette tell how she had spent the night, Master Devil took off at his very topmost speed for the nearly deserted town.

As he flew along, he put on a floppy straw hat, squeezed his hoofs into pointy-toed shoes, and covered his furry hide with a raggedy cloak. When he reached the town, he went to the neighborhood called Crochemort, a place frequented by some rough characters, the kind who don't say a lot, and don't need to. Their eyes had seen so much that they no longer distinguished between dream and reality. And they had so few illusions they were through asking questions of anyone, even of themselves. Among them was a skilled blacksmith who worked his iron with hammer and tongs, day and night.

"'Sdeath!" said the devil of gluttony. "Smooth out my tongue for me, my man, make it nice and thin. I'm singing at a wedding tonight, so I need a soft voice. I'll pay you thirty thousand sous for the job!" Without a word, the blacksmith grabbed a huge hammer, then unrolled the devil's massive tongue. At the sight of this object, which you can just imagine, the smith blinked once, heard four of his hairs turn white, but kept his mouth shut. He began to hammer this tongue, and he kept on hammering until he couldn't hammer anymore.

This took all day and all night. When the pippiree bird began to sing, the devil paid the bill and flew non-stop to the rock. Standing before Nanie-Rosette's little sanctuary, he swallowed a few blackbirds to pluck up his courage, and sang "*Nanie-Rosette mwen di'w*" over and over without teasing a single click-clack out of all those bolts and the dreaded deadlock. You would have thought that door had been nailed shut. Well, our devil didn't mope about. Glancing at the sun, he knew it would be a little while before the mother showed up again, and in the time it takes me to tell you about it, he had landed back at the smithy in Crochemort.

"'Sblood!" shouted the devil. "My voice still isn't soft enough, my friend. Make my tongue as thin as a piece of cardboard—no, as thin as a sheet of paper. Sixty thousand sous to clinch the deal!" This time the blacksmith didn't blink an eye or turn a hair. He shrugged off his shirt, stirred up a fine blaze, and beat that tongue with a hammer gone mad. Tonk! Tonk! Tonk! He was sweating like a pig on a spit. Soon the tongue was parchment-thin, like a banana leaf dried crisp in the sun. After the devil had paid, the blacksmith warned him not to eat anything before he sang. "*Tention boug, pa valé ayen douvan lè bay la vwa'w!*" But the devil of gluttony had already set out for that miserable rock.

Once there, and savoring his inevitable victory, he took the time to squat, mop his brow, and gobble (just a snack) the rancid leftovers from the spoiled celebration of two nights before, which dainties had been stashed in the shade of a clump of grass. So his chops were all greasy when he sang "*Nanie-Rosette mwen di'w,*" and he sang it in vain. "My voice is still too thick," he thought. Picking handfuls of big leaves, he wiped off his lips and gums (which is why, to this very day, the undergrowth in our woods is full of succulents). Off in the distance, the footsteps of the mama could be heard rustling through groves of bamboo as she hurried to the rock with the rest of the townspeople. The devil cleared his throat, unfurled his slenderized tongue, and sang:

> *Nanie-Rosette mwen di'w*
> *Nanie-Rosette dita Rosette dita Rosette*
> *Sé mwen Nanie*
> *Bagui di, bagui di, quin!*
> *Sé mwen Nanie, dita Rosette*

The first time she heard the song, Nanie-Rosette flipped the thirteen flat bolts. The second time, she pulled the thirteen sliding bolts. But the third time, since the devil had not been able to resist greedily gulping down a butterfly fluttering by, Nanie-Rosette detected in his voice the rasping growl of hell. And the deadlock never budged while Nanie-Rosette shot back all the other bolts.

And now the devil of gluttony lost his temper. He stooped to a trick that was snake-belly low. From the magic of his stomach came forth aromas of freshly baked bread, the spicy perfume of pimento sauces, the appetizing smells of colombo curries, ragouts, grilled fish with sauce chien, salt meat with beans, and the clatter of cake pans and ice cream makers. Clack-click-clack! Nanie-Rosette flipped the flat bolts, pulled the sliding bolts, and thinking only of her vice (without even pausing to reflect that her mama would never find the ghost of a trace of her and that the werewolves and fiends would have a gala feast that night), she undid the deadlock and threw the door wide open.

BOOK DESIGN AND PREPARATION BY CHARLES NIX